DOROTHY SALISBURY DAVIS

"Dashiell Hammett, Raymond Chandler and Josephine Tey . . . Dorothy Salisbury Davis belongs in the same company. She writes with great insight into the psychological motivations of all her characters." —*The Denver Post*

"Dorothy Salisbury Davis may very well be the best mystery novelist around." —*The Miami Herald*

"Davis has few equals in setting up a puzzle, complete with misdirection and surprises." —*The New York Times Book Review*

"Davis is one of the truly distinguished writers in the medium; what may be more important, she is one of the few who can build suspense to a sonic peak." —Dorothy B. Hughes, *Los Angeles Times*

"A joyous and unqualified success." —*The New York Times* on *Death of an Old Sinner*

"An intelligent, well-written thriller." —*Daily Mirror* on *Death of an Old Sinner*

"At once gentle and suspenseful, warmly humorous and tensely perplexing." —*The New York Times* on *A Gentleman Called*

"Superbly developed, gruesomely upsetting." —*Chicago Tribune* on *A Gentleman Called*

"An excellent, well-controlled piece of work." —*The New Yorker* on *The Judas Cat*

"A book to be long remembered." —*St. Louis Post-Dispatch* on *A Town of Masks*

"Mrs. Davis has belied the old publishing saying that an author's second novel is usually less good than the first. Since her first ranked among last year's best, what more need be said?" —*The New York Times* on *The Clay Hand*

"Ingeniously plotted ... A story of a young woman discovering what is real in life and in herself." —*The New York Times* on *A Death in the Life*

"Davis brings together all the elements needed for a good suspense story to make this, her fourth Julie Hayes, her best." —*Library Journal* on *The Habit of Fear*

"Mrs. Davis is one of the admired writers of American mystery fiction, and *Shock Wave* is up to her best. She has a cultured style, handles dialogue with a sure ear, and understands people better than most of her colleagues." —*The New York Times Book Review* on *Shock Wave*

A Gentleman Called

A Gentleman Called

A Mrs. Norris Mystery

Dorothy Salisbury Davis

All rights reserved, including without limitation the right to reproduce this book or any portion thereof in any form or by any means, whether electronic or mechanical, now known or hereinafter invented, without the express written permission of the publisher.

This is a work of fiction. Names, characters, places, events, and incidents either are the product of the author's imagination or are used fictitiously. Any resemblance to actual persons, living or dead, businesses, companies, events, or locales is entirely coincidental.

Copyright © 1958 by Dorothy Salisbury Davis

Cover design by Tracey Dunham

ISBN 978-1-4804-6042-3

This edition published in 2014 by Open Road Integrated Media, Inc.
345 Hudson Street
New York, NY 10014
www.openroadmedia.com

A Gentleman Called

1

Mrs. Norris fastened the last bit of sheeting around the legs of the last chair in the room to be covered, and then rechecked the whole of the hooded furniture for snugness. It was not that she expected wind—or for that matter, a windless occupancy—in the shuttered house. But neither would she have ruled out the possibility of the latter, especially in this room where the late General Jarvis had in his day stirred up so much fury.

The housekeeper gave a great sigh which, finally admitting the truth to herself at least, she acknowledged to have been sent after her late employer. There was many a man walking this earth of whom it could be said he was more dead than alive, but not many in their graves of whom you could say they were more alive than dead: the spirit was strong, however weak had been the flesh. She double-checked the locks on the windows and then went quickly from the room, clutching her skirts in her hand as though to be sure all of her got out at once and closed the door.

On the whole she was glad young Mr. Jarvis had decided to close the Nyack house for the winter. A Fifth Avenue apartment overlooking Central Park was not to be complained of by its housekeeper. True, she would miss the Hudson River which she often thought better company than some of the people she knew. But it was always cranky in November, the river, and rude as winter itself to all her acquaintance who didn't live near it. Mr. Tully, for example—her friend the detective, as she called him, not being able quite at her age to call him her beau, and having a deep aversion to the phrase "gentleman friend," as though she would have a male caller who was not a gentleman—Mr. Tully when he came at all this weather, would take up a stance before the fire the minute he gave up his topcoat, and turn himself round and round like a hare on a spit until it was time to go home.

Which but showed, she decided on further thought while she rolled up the hall rug, how little adaptability there was in the man. City born and city bred, he would not be transplanted at his age. She wondered then if her Master Jamie had taken into consideration Mr. Tully's attentions to her, in making his own change of winter residence.

Now here was a man—her Mister James—perceptive and considerate, and himself marvelously adaptable. He could oblige fortune and fame, or he could brook failure with the dignity of a royal pretender. He was in fact all things to at least one woman. Mrs. Norris had raised him the forty-odd years of his life.

Downstairs, she paused at the library door and asked if there was any way in which she could help him. He was packing his own books.

"Do you have the measurement of the shelves in town?"

She liked the way the words "in town" slipped from his tongue. It took out whatever sting there was for her in the change. She measured the largest of the books by the breadth of her own hand.

"They'll fit well enough, sir, but are you taking them all?"

"Those I need," he said.

She started from the room, but could not resist a further plea though she knew the cause lost as far as coming between him and his books was concerned. "Don't you have the law books at the office, Mr. James?"

"Yes," he said, continuing to pack law books.

She waited a moment at the door. "I left your father's den to the last and it's done now. I have only to gather up my own few bits and pieces."

"My God," said Jimmie, "if you feel that bad, we'd better stop for a drink."

"I don't feel that bad at all," Mrs. Norris said.

"Then you don't want a drink?"

"I didn't say that. I'll not be made out a hypocrite, Mr. James."

Jimmie rubbed his chin with a dirty thumb. Certainly not

if it meant doing her out of a drink at the same time. "Will you bring in the makings, then, Mrs. Norris?"

"I will since you ask it."

When she returned with the tray, Jimmie said: "I don't suppose Jasper will take it at all hard, your moving into the city?" There was a bit of the tease in him his father had been.

"It's very difficult to tell," Mrs. Norris said. "Mr. Tully's a cool man for an Irishman."

"I'd never have known it hearing him speak your praises," Jimmie said slyly.

Mrs. Norris gave her shoulders a vigorous shrugging. "I was speaking of his blood, not his blather."

"Blather," Jimmie repeated, wiping his hands on the duster she gave him. "Isn't that an Irish word?"

"It is a Gaelic word, Master James, and there were Gaels in Scotland while Ireland was a circle of druids."

Jimmie laughed. "I wonder what your friend Tully would say to that."

"He would agree likely. Mr. Tully is not a contentious man when it comes to nationalities."

"True enough," said Jimmie, for he knew Jasper Tully well. That long, melancholy detective was chief investigator in the District Attorney's office, and had been through many administrations, including Jimmie's own a few years past. He poured Mrs. Norris her usual finger of Scotch whiskey straight and mixed himself one with soda. "Do you still call him Mister Tully to his face also?" he teased. "You've known him for quite a while now."

Mrs. Norris pulled an extra inch of height from her dumpy shape. "I don't approve the informality in the world today, Mr. James. It's made strangers of us all."

Jimmie thought about it and then nodded acquiescence. He gave her her glass and lifted his own. He was a long moment contemplating the toast that was to be given on this occasion. It might be said that he was abandoning the house in which he had been born. Abandoning it or escaping it and the man whose personality marked it more deeply than had his own.

"To father," he said at last. "May he rest in peace."

Mrs. Norris paused in the act of lifting the glass to her lips. "I'm not at all certain he would have said 'amen' to that, Master Jamie."

"Then, being his sole heir and executor, I shall say it for him," Jimmie said, and added in gentle irony: "Prithy peace, amen."

The late Ransom Jarvis, retired major general of the United States Army, had left an estate of three dollars and seventeen cents.

2

The following Monday morning Jimmie commenced the pattern of what he expected to set as daily routine: the reading of The New York Times at breakfast, the walk to the Lexington Avenue subway, and the reading of the Herald Tribune on the ride downtown to the Wall Street office of Johnson, Wiggam and Jarvis.

All his life he had enjoyed the setting of patterns—almost as much as he enjoyed breaking them. He had served in many capacities for a man his age, most of which had at one time or other benefited by his having been trained in the Law. He wondered if, now that he was determined to confine himself to its practice, his novitiate to politics would benefit him. He thought it likely. He had been defeated recently as candidate for governor of the state. And never had he stood so well with the very senior and very proper members of the law firm.

An unsuccessful candidacy for high political office had certain things to recommend it, he mused. More to the respectable citizenry than, say, retirement from that high office. It might be implied, albeit the matter was insusceptible of proof, that the unsuccessful candidate had been above the making of deals. Impotence therein shone as virtue. Meanwhile it was patently obvious that no one fresh out of office had any right-of-way whatever in traffic with those who had succeeded him. But he was expected to run that way all the same, and was therefore damned twice for but one failure.

Shakespeare could have made a sonnet of that, Jimmie thought, and turned to the editorial page.

His secretary greeted him with too much cheer for a Monday morning. He expected bad news. With his mail she brought him word that Mr. Wiggam was waiting to see him on a matter of urgency.

"Urgency?" Jimmie repeated. It was a word rarely used in the office.

"He came to your office himself," the girl amended.

The placement of his office at the opposite end of the floor from the senior partners' was a source of irritation to Jimmie. "He likes to take long walks in the morning," he said. He was not long, however, in answering Wiggam's summoning.

Mr. Wiggam gave the first few seconds to a visual appraisal of the junior member of the firm. The wistful lingering of his eyes on Jimmie's midriff suggested one of two things: either he would have liked to see what there was of it encased in a vest and bound by a watch chain, or he was being nostalgic after his own lean-bellied days. Finally he inquired after Mrs. Norris. Still later he brought himself to the matter which, urgent or not, was obviously painful.

"Do you know the Adkins family?"

Jimmie furrowed his brow in thought.

"Weston, Connecticut. Particularly, have you heard of the son, Theodore Adkins?"

"Not to my recollection," Jimmie said.

"Very old family. Georgianna—the mother—has been a friend of my family for years." Wiggam drew a deep breath. "The boy—Teddy, that is—has got himself into something. A paternity action has been brought against him."

Small wonder Wiggam was pained. Johnson, Wiggam and Jarvis refused divorce cases. Jimmie thought it duly retributive that such a case as this be thrust upon them. But he pulled a long face.

"Teddy is a bachelor," Wiggam proceeded, "a condition which, I suppose, makes him susceptible to this sort of thing."

Jimmie, himself a bachelor, said: "Married men are even more susceptible, for which I suppose society should be grateful."

Wiggam cleared his throat. "I referred to the susceptibility to blackmail. And that's what it is, whether or not he's the father of this bastard." He seemed to take a great deal of satisfaction out of the specifics of language, Jimmie thought.

"He will contest the suit?" he asked.

"I should certainly expect him to," Wiggam said. "That is a matter to be worked out between him and counsel."

"I take it you have accepted the retainer?" Jimmie said, scoring every point now that he could for himself.

"I could not do anything else," Wiggam said sharply. "The man's mother and mine went to school together."

That gave Jimmie some pause. He had thought they were talking of someone young and hot-blooded. "How old is Teddy-boy?"

Mr. Wiggam winced. "Mid-fifties, I suppose."

Jimmie made a quick calculation of the age of a mother of a lad of fifty-five. Wiggam was not easily cowed. A dowager Lysistrata, by the sounds of it.

"Fine woman, his mother. You will want to meet her," Wiggam said brightly, confirming thereby Jimmie's worst premonitions.

"I doubt it," Jimmie said. "I assume from your confidence, sir, I am to take on the defense?"

"Johnson and I are convinced that without your active return to the firm, we could not have undertaken it, and Georgianna would never have understood our position."

"Does she understand her son's position?" Jimmie asked, intending the question to be taken as rhetorical.

"She is not an unworldly woman, Jim. You will have no trouble understanding one another."

Jimmie grinned. "I wondered which of my qualities recommended me to this assignment. My worldliness, is that it?"

Wiggam said it with a straight face: "Precisely. Your sensitivity to the areas of what I may call 'plunder,' the plunder by one man of another's privacy."

It was not a lecture Jimmie needed to attend. He had made copy for more than one gossip columnist in his career. The remarks, however, told him obliquely the extent of Mr. Wiggam's bias in the case, a bias natural enough to a man of his peculiar social consciousness.

"You would not allow the complainant any merit to her suit?"

"Certainly not," Wiggam said.

"Has she money?"

"I have no notion. I should think not or she could not expect to win out over respectability. Deprivation is her only plea, deprivation suing plenty. And she will, of course, insist upon a jury trial, praying that that prospect will force you into a settlement."

"Are you sure you're not her advocate, sir?"

Wiggam was not amused.

"When do I meet our client?" Jimmie said.

"This evening. I have suggested that he call on you at home tonight—or as soon as you can conveniently see him there. I consider it a matter too delicate for the office."

It was Jimmie's turn to be not amused. Such availability had not been in his scheme of things when he decided on a city residence for winter.

3

Mrs. Norris had been expecting Mr. Tully to dinner that evening; she had laid in an excellent steak for him only to have him phone in the late afternoon and offer the most mournful of regrets. A policeman's lot: murder for his dinner. She wished him a 'good appetite' that was neither tart nor sweet, taking herself a certain relish in the less sordid aspects of Mr. Tully's business. She suggested that he might stop by for a cup of tea if he were able to make it before midnight.

She turned then to the refinements of settling the new household, the arrangement of the silver in the butler's pantry. Mr. James was out to dinner. He expected a caller at nine o'clock and if he was not himself home then, Mrs. Norris had her instructions. At two minutes after nine the doorman phoned up to say that Mr. Adkins was in the elevator. Mrs. Norris washed her hands.

When she opened the door to him he was standing like something fresh out of a box, a bald, shining little man, scarcely taller than herself, his skin a scrubbed pink, his eyes almost a mad blue, they were so bright and lively. Whether he lingered those thirty seconds to appraise her or to be himself appraised, it would have been hard to say. No doubt of it, he liked to make an impression. And he had succeeded.

"Mr. Jarvis expects me, madam. I am Theodore Adkins."

Glimpsing in the mirror his passage down the hall after her, his balance seeming to settle in his heels with every step, Mrs. Norris was reminded of a penguin. A pleasant enough bird, she reasoned, if you didn't have to do its laundry.

"Mr. Jarvis will be home very soon, sir," she said, throwing open the library door. "He bade me set the fire in here for you and offer his apologies if he was delayed. Can I bring you something?"

Mr. Adkins drew a chair closer to the blazing fire and settled himself like a nesting bird before answering. He turned a cherubic face up into hers. "What would you suggest?"

"Brandy?" The burr native so many years before to her tongue turned up again at that instant, her having taken a slight pique at the man's leisure with her time as well as his own.

"By my soul, you're Scotch!" he cried.

"I am." Her antagonism vanished. She dearly loved being discovered for what she was.

The man made a lacework of fingers far too delicate for the stomach over which he entwined them. "When I was a boy I knew Highlands and Lowlands. I had a governess who finished off prayers with me every night with a verse you might find familiar:

'From ghouls and ghosties
And three legged hosties
And things that go bump in the night
The Lord deliver us...'"

Mr. Adkins smiled ruefully and shook his head. "I don't know what it was that the Lord delivered me from in answer to her prayers, but do you know, I've taken an inordinate degree of pleasure ever since in things that go bump in the night?"

What a delightful man, Mrs. Norris thought. "You might like a glass of port, sir," she suggested. "I've heard Mr. James recommend it to the real connoisseurs."

"Will you have a glass with me?"

"No, sir, I will not," she said, and with genuine regret that a man of such obvious high station should show such low taste.

He popped to his feet and gave a deep bow. "Forgive the familiarity, dear lady. Something in the moment brought me back to the company of my own Miss Ramsey."

"I am a widow," Mrs. Norris said, her emphasis on the word making the distinction between herself and his own Miss Ramsey even stronger.

"Of a sea captain," Mr. Adkins cried.

"He was a man of the sea," she admitted in some awe of the inner sight the man must possess.

"And lost at sea, wasn't he?"

"Aye, sir, a long time ago."

"And you've been faithful to his memory all these years," he said with an awesome respect.

"He gave me no reason to forget him, poor boy," Mrs. Norris chimed, aware of growing lugubrious. The truth was that he had given her little reason to remember him either.

"Then he did leave you provided for," Mr. Adkins said.

Mrs. Norris lifted her chin. "Aye. With a sea bag to pack my duds in."

Mr. Adkins blinked his eyes at her in mute admiration. "I shall have the port, thank you."

The tastefulness and timeliness of his dismissal thereby recovered for him completely the esteem he had lost so early. He was merely impetuous, impetuous and open-hearted, Mrs. Norris decided, and she wondered—as she rarely did of his affairs—on what business Mr. James was seeing this remarkable man.

4

Jimmie reached home just before nine-thirty. His first impression of his client was that he was a modest, conservative man. Not too modest, perhaps, Jimmie second-thought the matter: his clothes were cut to compensate nature's mismanagements. But Adkins, surprised in the act of refilling his own glass, actually blushed.

"How do you do, sir," Jimmie said, extending his hand. "Mrs. Norris, I see, has made my excuses."

"Indeed she has. I might almost wish you longer delayed—with her company and this." He held up the glass. "One might wonder which had been with you the longer." He sighed and shook his head. "Wine and women, I should not mix them even in metaphor."

Jimmie laughed.

"Oh, my dear man," Adkins cried, "I hope you laugh because my situation is not desperate?"

"From what I can gather, your situation at its worst could be scarcely desperate, Mr. Adkins. You are not a married man?"

"Certainly not."

"That is the sort of circumstance that might make a situation such as yours desperate," Jimmie said.

"I am rather jealous of my reputation, Jarvis, and I cannot see this sort of legal action as improving it. That is why, for my part, I should like to see the thing settled out of court."

"The plaintiff mentions a hundred thousand dollars as a sum she would consider settling for on behalf of her son—which amount, in turn, she would be happy to have you invest. . ."

"I am a broker," Adkins said.

"She would like a guaranteed income of five thousand a year from it," Jimmie went on.

Adkins threw back his head and laughed much too heartily. "Oh, my dear Jarvis, if you but knew the irony of that!" He was serious then. "I don't have a hundred thousand dollars. My mother has several millions, but not I."

Jimmie somehow wanted to delay a discussion of the Dowager Adkins as long as possible. "Miss Daisy Thayer—the plaintiff—and if it does come to trial I ought to be able to do something with that name before a jury—seems to have an extraordinary memory. It would seem she has almost total recall of the incidents of your relationship." Jimmie had spent the afternoon going over the particulars in the bill.

"Oh, the wretch!" Adkins cried.

"How old is Miss Thayer, by the way?"

Adkins thought about it. "I'm not very good at gauging the ages of women. My mother seems ageless and my sisters perennial. I should say Daisy is anywhere between twenty-five and forty."

"That puts her within the age of consent at least," Jimmie said dryly. A blind man could draw a better sight than that on a woman.

"Oh yes," Mr. Adkins said quite seriously.

"You seem to have made several proposals to her—in writing and it would seem on tape recording—that suggest serious intentions, a permanent relationship."

"I had something of that sort in mind, all right," Adkins admitted.

"Matrimony?"

"Matrimony is not very permanent in our concupiscent times, is it?" Adkins said earnestly. "But no doubt I suggested it, nonetheless."

"To what purpose?" Jimmie said. "That's what the jury will want to know."

Adkins folded his hands and smiled, a flashing beatific sort of smile that suggested a very unworldly man. "No doubt," he said.

Since his answers were ambiguous, Jimmie put his questions the more directly. "Do you think you're the father of—what's its name—Alexander?"

"Certainly not."

"You did not have relations with the woman?"

"I did not."

Jimmie sighed. It was not going to be easy to make a persuasive argument to that effect in face of Miss Thayer's memories. Yet there was something about Adkins to give credence to his words, an aura, an attitude, something, to put it bluntly, virginal. But try to get that across to a jury!

"You mentioned wanting to make a settlement out of court," Jimmie said. "What did you have in mind?"

"Why," Adkins said, "I suppose I'd be willing to be say, godfather to the child."

"I somehow doubt that that will satisfy his mother," Jimmie said. "And I'm just afraid you and I are going to have to go over some of the details of your relationship, Mr. Adkins. It's rather important that at least I understand your position."

Adkins nodded. Then he asked brightly, "Would you like to know how I met her?"

"All right," Jimmie said, but he excused himself first and got a wine glass from the cabinet. He filled his own glass and added a half to Teddy Adkins'. The little man's cheeks were peony red, and he had himself a baby sort of face. Very good timing on Miss Thayer's part to bring suit at this age of her child's: hold any baby of six to twelve months up next to Teddy Adkins, and you were bound to strike a resemblance. "You were going to tell me about meeting Miss Thayer," Jimmie prompted.

"I was. She worked—and I believe still does—in the perfume department of one of our better stores, Mark Stewart's. It was midsummer, a year ago last July probably. I remember how enormously cool she looked..."

And calculating, Jimmie thought.

"The perfume counter adjoins umbrellas," Adkins went on. "I have never in my adult life been able to resist the perusal of an umbrella counter. Nor, for that matter, a perfume counter, although until that occasion, I had managed to observe the latter from a safe distance."

Jimmie smiled. At least Adkins had a sense of humor about it, and he was going to need it.

"I remember now that she spoke first, said something about having an umbrella like the one at which I was looking. She advised me against the purchase of it. Said the knob always came off in her hand. I said some damned nonsense about its not being difficult to lose one's knob in her hands..." He blushed now at the recollection. "Not every man is gifted with the prophecy of his own doom, eh, Jarvis? I invited her to lunch...and learned a great deal about perfumes. I even thought a bit about manufacturing them. I putter a bit with one thing and another. Making things, you know. A restless sort of man, I am." Adkins sighed. "But I thought then of Mama. I must take her into consideration every move. Having raised three daughters in tweeds while despairing first of a male heir and then of his survival, she could not be expected to take kindly to his careering in perfumes."

There was the crux of the matter, Jimmie thought, and wondered if Adkins knew it of himself.

"Now I hope this won't shock you, Jarvis, but I am most anxious not to displease Mama. I have not yet come into my inheritance, and despite evidence to the contrary, I do not believe she can live forever."

And still it was not Mama's age but Teddy-boy's that Jimmie had to sometimes remind himself of. "I consider myself fortunate," Jimmie said, interjecting a personal note, "in having been cured of such expectancy at the age of sixteen. My father borrowed ten dollars from me that I had just won in an oratory contest. To my recollection, he never did pay it back."

"You can, at least, remember your father," Adkins said.

"Oh yes," said Jimmie. "It would be hard not to. I wonder if we could now go into some of the particulars in your relationship."

"I suppose sooner or later we must get down to the sordid aspects," Adkins said dismally. "And it was all so beautiful in the beginning."

Jimmie glanced at him sharply, wondering if he were sincere. Apparently he was. Jimmie consulted his notes. "Did you on August 3, 1956, write a letter in which occurred the words: 'I feel I must approach the holy day as was the custom in olden times when matrimony was a sacrament. I shall want a few days in solitary contemplation, in retreat.'

And then later in the letter: 'In bond I shall love you out of all bounds.'"

Adkins had gone a deep red. "I wrote it," he said quietly.

"Beautiful," Jimmie said.

His client brightened. "I thought so myself."

Jimmie cleared his throat and turned to another page. "The tape recording—you know what that contains?"

Adkins almost flew from the chair and began to pace the room. "Oh, yes. Despicable wench, to have turned it to such ill use! I should think that in civilized society the very presentment of such evidence would mitigate against her."

"I hope that will happen, Mr. Adkins," Jimmie said. "Now Miss Thayer recalls that you spent the night of August 5 with her..."

"The evening, not the night," Adkins interrupted.

"Do you remember it?"

"Quite distinctly. It was a full moon when I drove home."

"I don't suppose the man in the moon is an unfriendly witness," Jimmie said, "but I doubt that he'll be much help. Do you suppose anyone else could testify to seeing you that night?"

Adkins shook his head. "I am solitary in my habits. I doubt it."

"Did you and Miss Thayer exchange any mementos of your affections for each other?"

Adkins who had been standing before the fireplace whirled about on Jimmie. "What?"

Jimmie repeated his question.

"What, may I ask, suggests that, Mr. Jarvis?"

Jimmie shrugged, unable to understand the turn that seemed to have given his client. "I was trying to find evidence of cupidity on the part of Miss Thayer. I should think she might have tried to get a ring or some token she might use as a pledge from you."

Adkins flashed a smile, a beamish boy, Jimmie thought. "Forgive me, Jarvis. I mistook you to be questioning my integrity. As a matter of fact she did ask me for a token. It came out of our conversation one evening, I think—she asked me if she might have my army 'dog tag' to keep for sentiment."

"And did you give it to her?" Jimmie said, leaning forward.

"Yes. I had a devil of a time finding it, but I managed."

"And does she have it now?"

"Oh no. It came back when we parted."

"Could you tell me the circumstances under which you parted?"

"We quarreled one night over something trivial—and likely distasteful. A rather vulgar girl, Daisy, when one got to know her. As a matter of fact when I was leaving she told me then she was in a position to—to do what she has just done."

That, Jimmie thought, was a very roundabout way of saying that Daisy had told him she was pregnant. Squeamish as well as beamish, Mr. Adkins.

"What did you say to her then, Mr. Adkins?"

The little man threw up his hands. "I told her to do it, by all means. I assumed it to be a wishful sort of bluff."

"Have you any idea why she wanted your army 'dog tag'?"

"At the time it was, well, like an intimate bit of apparel. Or so I thought. A bit of animal, there is in that girl, Jarvis."

"There is indeed," said Jimmie, "the vixen. A piece of vital information came to her by that tag: your blood type. And if, as you say, you are not the father of the child, she must have shopped to your specifications."

Adkins made a round mouth of shocked surprise. "For a...a..."

"That's right," Jimmie said. "If you've been framed, it has been done in proper style. I don't suppose you knew any other young men of her acquaintance at the time?"

"Oh, no. I was not competitive," Adkins said.

"And would anyone else know of your having given her your 'dog tag'?"

Adkins thought about that. "My sister, Miranda, would know of my having looked for it at the time. It was she had it, and no small business was it to get it from her either. She's rather possessive about me, you see. But naturally I did not tell her for whom I wanted it."

After threshing through, but not out, other incidents of Mr. Adkins's relationship with the woman, Jimmie tried to put the alternatives in the case before his client. "We may in the end have to pay something to keep it from going to trial," he said. "Would you consider doing that?"

"I would, but Mama would not. As a matter of fact, Jarvis, this whole thing seems to be giving her an inordinate amount of pleasure. It seems to have rejuvenated her, and to tell the truth, I had rather counted on it to have the opposite effect. She has become a naughty old woman. And I am just afraid it is you who will have to deal with her. After all you are *her* lawyers, Wiggam and all of you."

Adkins seemed to be going to pieces at the very mention of his mother. It confirmed Jimmie's suspicions of the woman. He gave a great sigh himself. He was getting a little old to deal with the vigors of her generation. "She will see me?"

"Noblesse oblige," Adkins said.

5

Jasper Tully was indeed a melancholy man at having to pass up Mrs. Norris' invitation to dinner. A widower, he lived in the Bronx with his sister whose cooking, like her conversation, was composed of scraps she had picked up and flavored to her own taste.

But the report of homicide which had come through to the District Attorney's office late that November afternoon located the incident in the upper east Nineties, a neighborhood congested and inflammable with a new minority people pressing in upon an old minority, and in their midst, trying to withstand both pressures, were a few resident holdouts of second or third generation New Yorkers in the once elegant brownstones. To these latter, the victim, Mrs. Arabella Sperling, belonged. The District Attorney thought his chief investigator ought to be on hand.

Tully sometimes wondered if all the Precinct and Homicide men who answered a complaint were necessary. He was in favor of science if it didn't get in the way of reason. But then, the younger men didn't need room to think. Left alone, they couldn't think their way through a railroad flat. Teamwork. It was all a matter of teamwork. Tully slithered his way through the team and its equipment to the room from which the victim's body had been recently removed. He talked with the Medical Examiner who had waited for him.

The woman had been dead for about forty-eight hours, apparently strangled to death in her bed, and likely in her sleep, for there had been no struggle at all. Her throat had been neatly and deeply massaged by someone who knew his anatomy.

Tully looked then at the double bed from which the technical men were about to remove the linens.

"Anybody sleep in that with her?" he asked.

Lieutenant Greer, who was in charge of the investigation, stood by also. He was at the frustrating stage of the investigation where everything remained to be done and nothing could be done immediately: men were searching for physical evidence, others for witnesses, without having turned up enough of anything yet to justify action.

"Not regularly," he said in answer to Tully's question.

Tully observed the salvaging and preservation of a long gray hair. "How old a woman?"

"Fifty-one, according to her insurance policies."

"Who's the beneficiary?"

"Two nieces," Greer said. "Very unlikely suspects."

"Got any likely ones?"

Greer looked at him with a jaded tolerance. "Give us an hour or two, will you, Tully?" He led the way then to the dressing table; a film of fingerprint powder lay over much of it. "There was robbery. This jewel box was emptied. But no sign of housebreaking. And herself sleeping peacefully in bed."

"Herself not surprised," murmured Tully. "Who made the complaint?"

"The building superintendent. When the newspapers accumulated in the hall from a couple of days, he remembered that she was in the habit of telling him if she expected to be away overnight. That's his story. She owned this building, and he has a key to the apartment. But—he got a cop to come with him before entering."

"The careful sort, isn't he?" said Tully.

"I'd say that. But maybe that's how you get living in this neighborhood."

"He lives in the house?"

"Across the street. It's the only other building in this block the new ones haven't got into yet."

The new ones, Tully mused. He had heard them called worse, God knows. "I take it he isn't one of the—new ones?"

"He's a white man, Johanson. A Swede, I'd say."

"Have you got a statement from him?"

"Only what the lad took who made the complaint with

him. I wanted to know as much as I could about what happened in this room before tackling him. I've got an idea he's going to be a very cagey fellow."

When he met Johanson himself a few minutes later, Tully agreed with the detective's estimate. Shrewd or slow-witted, it was hard to tell at first. But Johanson measured his every answer before giving it. Mrs. Sperling's building was the furthest uptown he worked.

"I have good addresses, my other buildings," he said. "Fifth Avenue, Park Avenue, and I get good references from any of them I can tell you. I am a reliable man."

Tully was sure he would have good references, making that point of it. He sat back and listened to Greer's questioning.

"How long have you worked for Mrs. Sperling?"

"Five years last April," the man said slowly.

"How often are you in this building?"

"Every morning I come here at six o'clock. Because I live across the street I come here first. At five o'clock in the afternoon, wintertime, I come also. It is a very old furnace in the basement."

"Did you see Mrs. Sperling regularly?"

"I do not know what you call regular, sir. One day I saw her and maybe not the next. I would see her at least two or three times a week."

"In her apartment?"

"No, sir. In the vestibule."

Tully marked his own notes: that the victim had occupied the first floor apartment.

"When were you last in her apartment?" Greer asked.

"Not ever until I went in with the officer."

"Didn't Mrs. Sperling interview you before hiring you?"

"Yes, sir. In my own living-room across the street."

"It doesn't seem just right, you having a key and never being in this apartment in five years' employment. Don't things go wrong with the plumbing in these old houses?"

"Sure. But Mrs. Sperling, she was a very handy woman."

"She must have been," the lieutenant said sourly. He enquired then about the other tenants, eliciting nothing that seemed pertinent to Tully. Then he asked about any visitors Johanson had ever encountered with Mrs. Sperling.

"I've been thinking about that," the man said. "Now I could tell, Lieutenant, you don't believe me when I say Mrs. Sperling was a handy woman. I don't like to be called a liar by anybody. You listen to this—all of you." He looked about to include Tully and the police stenographer.

Tully nodded solemnly. Greer's nerves were not as steady. "Get on with it," he snapped.

"One morning about three weeks ago," Johanson proceeded at his own deliberate pace, "I found a leak in the joint of one of the furnace pipes. The pipes were knocking. There was a note to me in Mrs. Sperling's handwriting about how I should fix it first thing. Now that pipe, Lieutenant, ran along the basement ceiling, and it goes up through the floor into her apartment. I was trying to fix it, but I could not do it alone, you understand. And being up high where I was on the ladder, I could hear voices in her apartment. I heard a man's voice. So

I went upstairs and I rang her bell, and her being in a night gown, I said maybe she would send down the gentleman to help me with the pipe."

Tully and Greer exchanged glances. The stenographer paused to blow his nose. But Johanson proceeded blandly, apparently to this day unaware of his lack of discretion. "She says, 'What man are you talking about? I've got the radio on.' And she came down to the basement and held that wrench for me herself. But I didn't hear the radio when her door was open or any more when it was closed till she went upstairs again and turned it on. That time I knew it was a radio. So, I don't like to be called a liar or a fool. I went home to my breakfast and I told my wife to bring it to me where I could look out of the window. At eight o'clock the man on the third floor left. I know him, he is the tenant. At twenty minutes to nine, the man on the second floor left and his wife with him. And then, by God. . ." Johanson slapped the flat of his hand on his knee. . ."at nine-thirty out comes the man who wasn't there at all!"

He looked from one to the other of the police in triumph.

"How do you know he wasn't the guest of one of the tenants?" Greer asked without a smile.

"I don't think Mrs. Sperling comes to the window and waves goodbye to other people's visitors, no sir, I don't."

"I want you to give me the exact date this occurred, Johanson."

"October twenty-one," he said with very little hesitation.

"It is the day after we turn the heat up ten degrees, and that is a very busy day with old furnaces."

"A very busy day," Greer said, "but you could sit and look out the window."

"My time is my own, sir. My contract, she calls for the job, not for the time I do the job."

"I wish I could say the same for mine," Tully drawled, getting up, and taking part for the first time. He could never understand the baiting of witnesses in the wake of significant testimony as Greer had just done with his man. His own feeling was that by implying disbelief, the inquisitor weakened the witness's concentration. He might thereby lose a detail almost as significant as the fact.

"What was the fellow like, her caller?"

Johanson relaxed. He even smiled at the picture started up in his mind by Tully's question. It must be very vivid to him.

"Why, he come down the steps real business-like, brief case under his arm, umbrella. Not very tall and kind of chubby, one way you look at him. Then he's not so plump, you look at him another way. Good clothes maybe do that. . ."

Tully nodded. He would have purred if that would have kept Johanson running on as smoothly.

"He was neat as a spool of thread. I don't just remember his face. But it's the feeling I got when I saw him I remember real clear. He walked kind of bouncey—like on springs and back on his heels." Johanson pounded one hand into the other. "A jim-dandy walking doll, that's what I would call him! Do you see what I mean?"

"I might if I saw the man," Tully said. "From that description, I just might at that. And I wouldn't be surprised if other witnesses can corroborate it."

By eleven o'clock that night, however, no other witnesses admitted having seen such a man in the vicinity of Mrs. Sperling's, and Tully decided he had done a day's duty. He could still reach Fifth Avenue and 78th Street before midnight.

6

"Now it wasn't such a bad story he told," Tully explained to Mrs. Norris while he turned the plate round and round. Chocolate cake with coconut frosting: he wouldn't get the coconut out of his teeth for a week. He had hoped for the steak, midnight or no. But the Scotch were always careful with meat.

"Would you rather have something else, Mr. Tully?"

"To tell you the truth, Mrs. Norris, cake is too delicate for my stomach at this hour. I need something rough and substantial after a day's work."

"I've just the thing that'll stick to your ribs," she said. "These chilly mornings I make the porridge the night before. It's sitting now warm in the pot."

"That'd be just grand," Tully said with grim cheer, and returned to the description of the investigation. "You see it's too neat, the story he told about this visitor, or maybe too bold. Every other witness we talked to tonight was shocked at the very suggestion of a man staying overnight in the woman's house. Mrs. Sperling seems to have been as careful a woman as, say, yourself."

"I wouldn't rule out the careful ones any more than I'd rule them in for it," Mrs. Norris volunteered with the porridge. "By which I mean a woman's a woman for all o' that. The careful ones are lonesomer than the free ones, if you know what I mean."

"Oh, I do," Tully said. "And they won't rule out the man Johanson described, but it's himself who looks like their best bet at the moment. The very way he went about discovering the body—having a policeman go in with him on his key to an apartment he swore he had never crossed the threshold of. If she wanted to keep him out, why did she allow him a key? And twice, when they were in the place, the officer he took with him had to call him on touching things around the place—as though he was deliberately trying to leave his prints on something which would in turn, account for any other prints the police might turn up of his."

"Take plenty of cream," Mrs. Norris said. "You're getting leaner all the time."

"It runs in the family," Tully said.

"What kind of a man is this Johanson?"

"He's a shrewd lad, Johanson is—forty, I'd say—good-looking in a rough, working-man way. He has a toothpick of a wife and no kids."

"I'm always suspicious of a married man who hasn't a family," Mrs. Norris said.

"Aye, if I didn't know more of human nature, I'd be myself. But one of the biggest rogues I know has a parcel of kids and a wife that adores him. She's waiting for him at the neck of the jug every time he gets out of it. Then there's another kid. And the kids themselves are little angels, one prettier than the other. Ah, I had a friend once, Jimmie Phelan, God rest him, and he used to say when he'd get a few drinks in him: 'Sure, Jasper, there's many a horse thief sired a saint all unbeknownst to himself.'"

"True," Mrs. Norris said, wetting the tea. "Do you think this Johanson is trying to throw suspicion on someone he knows?"

"Or on somebody he doesn't know. Somebody he's just seen once and remembered," Tully said. "Mind you, I may change my mind about this in the morning. But let me ask you, if you wanted to give a good description of a man—by which you wanted to convince us there was such a man—wouldn't you pick out one you'd seen somewhere that stuck in your mind?"

"I would and I could," Mrs. Norris said, and looked at Tully with deep admiration. "I saw him on the subway years ago, with dimples in his cheeks and his eyes blue and laughing. He was a Yorkshire man—on his way to Kansas City."

"On the subway is where to observe them," Tully said.

Mrs. Norris was lost in the recollection then. "And he called me 'lass.' I hadn't heard the word said like that in years."

"I'm not very keen on your speaking to strangers," he said.

"'Twas before I knew you. But don't you see, Mr. Tully, it proves exactly what you were saying: if I had to, this minute, conjure a face and a figure, there's the man, the perfect red herring!"

At that moment Jimmie knocked and put his head through the doorway of the butler's pantry.

"Come in, sir," said Mrs. Norris. "Mr. Tully has a brand new murder."

"Congratulations," said Jimmie. He came to the table and shook hands with the detective. "A crime of passion, I hope. And just before you make the arrest, I'd appreciate your recommending me to the suspect. My God, can't you give the man anything better to eat at this hour than a bowl of porridge?"

"It's what he wanted," Mrs. Norris said.

And while that was not the truth, the truth was that he no longer wanted anything else, so Tully agreed with her.

"Is your visitor gone, Mr. James?" his housekeeper inquired.

"For the time being, at least. What did you think of him, Mrs. Norris? What kind of trouble would you say he was in?" Jimmie winked at Tully, and while he was waiting her answer helped himself to the cake the detective had passed up.

"He's not the kind of man who wears his troubles on his sleeve," Mrs. Norris said after a moment's contemplation. "And I dare say he's easily taken advantage of, especially by women. I'd say he was the companion to an old witch of a mother who's outlived her usefulness in this world by fifty years." Seeing Jimmie grin, his housekeeper warmed to the subject. "She probably didn't pay a fig's worth of attention to him till she was widowed, and since then latched onto him like a snail. She'd not let an eligible woman near him for fear he'd marry. So I'd say, he's probably in trouble now with an ineligible one. There now. Do I get the sixty-four thousand dollars?"

Jimmie laughed. "Not tonight, but we'll give you a crack at it next week," he said. "You're a marvelously perceptive woman." He held his fork poised in the air a moment and looked at her. "Do you really think he's a lady's man?"

"I found him attractive," Mrs. Norris said.

"Did you now?" said Tully, and to Jimmie. "Who the hell is she talking about?"

"I will not have that language in my kitchen," Mrs. Norris said, although the occasion did not displease her.

"He's the scion of an old and important family," Jimmie said, "and the heir to a fortune when his mother lets go."

"There!" Mrs. Norris cried in triumph.

"That'd make any man attractive," Tully said, "to some women." Then seeing himself in deep waters, he added: "Present company excepted, of course."

"You don't know me very well to say that, Mr. Tully, or even to think it's flattery to me to say it. I know the worth of money, having earned my own, and I must say, an honest fortune is a rare thing."

Both men laughed. And presently, realizing what she had said, Mrs. Norris joined them. "In fact," she said, "the honester, the rarer."

7

What seemed to be the first break in the Sperling investigation came the next morning. A Third Avenue pawnbroker reported an attempt to unload a couple of pieces of feminine jewelry by a lad he seized and held for the police. Tully stopped at the precinct headquarters and heard John Thompson's story himself. By then what was presumed to be the rest of Mrs. Sperling's treasures had been surrendered by the boy. Since there was no insurance listing on them, they waited inventory by the two nieces.

Johnny was only fifteen and small for his age at that. As one of the cops said, Arabella would have had to give him a hand to help in her own strangulation. He claimed to have found the chamois bag containing the jewelry in the hallway of Mrs.

Sperling's house. He was a very frightened boy, getting more attention in ten minutes now, Tully thought, than in all the years of his life put together.

"In the first place, young fella," Tully said, "what were you doing in the hallway?"

"Readin' the comics," Johnny said. "Honest. Every day when I'd see *The News*es delivered there, I'd sneak up and read 'em before they was took in. You can ask the super. He kicked me out sometimes."

"And what took you so long to try to sell the jewelry? You found it the morning before yesterday, didn't you?"

The boy nodded. "I was hopin' there'd be a reward for findin' them. I watched the paper, the Lost and Found."

"And decided this morning that honesty didn't pay off quick enough," Tully finished the story.

The lad would not change that tale much, Tully knew. His methods were his best witnesses. Mrs. Sperling's costume pieces were unlikely to have been taken for their own value. A ruse, likely, and a poor one without the sign of housebreaking. A bit of muddying on the murderer's part.

Johanson also stayed with his story: that of having never crossed Mrs. Sperling's doorstep during her lifetime, and this despite the doubt cast on his word by information the Precinct men turned up. Johanson had numerous small investments in shoddy Harlem real estate. Furthermore, he admitted under intensive questioning, having approached Mrs. Sperling to join his investment syndicate.

Tully allowed himself an editorial comment aloud on

people who take exorbitant profit out of over-crowded housing.

"You do not say this is not honest," Johanson insisted. "I can name you a dozen operators in New York, respectable men, Park Avenue, Fifth Avenue, Wall Street, and they all have money in Harlem real estate."

"Sure, you're right," Lieutenant Greer agreed. It was not his place to question the business ethics of either Johanson or the Sperling woman. Maybe the information would be of value to Tully whose boss would be in charge if Johanson was brought to trial, but that day wasn't coming fast enough.

"Let's try to line up a couple of dates and hours," Tully said. "When was it you asked Mrs. Sperling if she would like to invest in real estate with you?"

"Two, three weeks ago," Johanson said sullenly.

"And you were standing outside her door when you did it?"

"No, sir. We were in the basement of her building. She made me explain it over to her twice. Then she said she would ask her broker."

"Her broker," Tully repeated. "Ever meet him?"

The building super shook his head.

"I want you to take time now and figure out the exact date this took place, this conversation in the basement," Tully said.

After much puzzling of the pocket calendar the detective gave him, Johanson concluded that it had been one week before.

"That's not two, three weeks," Tully said.

"The days don't go so fast in my work," Johanson said. "Now I tell you the truth, sir. I was afraid to tell you sooner. Then I realized you maybe seen her broker and he told you when she spoke to him about it. She told me 'no' on the investment the day after. That would be last Wednesday."

Lieutenant Greer and Tully exchanged a signal between them: the moment had come to spring a most damaging piece of information. Greer had that morning gone over Mrs. Sperling's finances with her bank. He now took over the questioning.

"On Monday you asked her to invest in slum real estate. How much money?"

"I do not call it slum real estate."

"All right. We won't call it slum money either. How much?"

"I asked her for a few thousand dollars. Eight percent I promised her. I told her to decide. She knew my books by then."

"Having gone over them in the basement. And this was Monday. On Wednesday she told you 'no.' Her broker did not consider it a good investment. But on Friday morning, Mrs. Sperling withdrew five thousand dollars in small bills from the Regency State Bank. And she told the cashier, volunteered the information, mind you, that her broker had recommended real estate investment, but that it had to be a cash transaction. . ."

If Johanson was not shocked at that information, Tully thought, he was giving more than an actor's performance: he had gone deadly pale and his mouth worked all through Greer's summation without ever a sound coming from him.

"That was Friday morning at about eleven o'clock. By eleven o'clock Friday night she was strangled to death in her bed. Her jewelry was stolen, but dropped in the hallway, conveniently to tempt a young punk to get himself into real trouble. But that five thousand dollars, that's not showing up. That's vanished, hasn't it? Where would you suggest we look for it, Johanson?"

Johanson shook his head.

"Then let me go on," Greer said, hammering every incident home. "On Saturday morning you called a Mr. John P. Snull and assured him you then had enough money to cover the investment commitment you had made to him."

"But that was a lie," Johanson shouted finally, and then having found his voice, managed to continue. "I did not have enough money, but I hoped to raise it by Monday. I can give you the names and addresses of three men I went to for that money on Saturday after I talked to him. I didn't get the money, but I went to them and asked. I offered my whole profit to them for that part of the money. Twelve percent I promised them."

"You didn't by any chance go back to Mrs. Sperling's house that day to try to change her mind?" Tully asked quietly.

Johanson whirled around on him. "No, sir, but I thought about doing it, and then I remembered the morning paper in the hallway not picked up, and I thought Ha! She does not want to be disturbed. She's got her little man with her again."

"Oh, yes," Greer said with heavy sarcasm. "That one."

But with very little change, Johanson told the same story over and over again throughout the day to whomever asked it, whether at police headquarters, in his own living-room, or in the basement of the house that had belonged to the murdered woman. There were an old kitchen table and a couple of chairs in the basement which might have been used for conference. Both Mrs. Sperling's and her superintendent's fingerprints showed up on the porcelain top of the table. But no evidence of any worth showed up in Johanson's favor. His only alibi for the night of the murder was his wife's word, and she finally admitted having fallen asleep before he had even gone to bed. Greer and the Homicide men were in favor of charging the man. Tully had his doubts still. And since, through his boss, he was in theory at least, the man with the last word, the arrest was not made.

It was with the restlessness of a prisoned animal that Tully moved from source to source of evidence. He watched Mrs. Sperling's two nieces finger greedily the jewels recovered from the pawnbroker and Johnny Thompson. They were hungry for inherited wealth, these two girls. They could not be more than thirty years old, either of them, but they had the look of having abandoned their hopes for marriage at puberty.

Having seen in his long life of police work, all degrees of wretchedness in human behavior, Tully was still most revolted by greed, and especially greed in a woman.

"Ladies," he said, curling his tongue around the word, "I wonder if you could tell us whether anything is missing."

One of the two snapped: "Five thousand dollars."

"I mean among the jewelry," Tully said.

They exchanged glances, and then fell to open and bitter argument between themselves as to what might have been there and wasn't, and then as to what other disposition Mrs. Sperling might have made of something herself. It occurred to Tully while this was going on that in all the investigation so far no clear picture was coming out at all of the victim. That was chiefly what was wrong. Nobody had been able—or maybe it just was that nobody was willing—to tell what kind of person Arabella Sperling had been. Did anybody, for example, call her Arabella, or just plain Bella? What had she thought of these two gulls scrabbling now over the remains?

They had reached a decision. Something was missing after all.

"A breast pin, a diamond 'lover's knot' in white gold," the spokeswoman of them said. "It belonged to our grandmother."

"Maybe she gave it to somebody," Tully suggested.

The twosome wagged their heads. "It was to come to us. Auntie Arabella was a fair woman."

Fair is foul, Tully thought, and took out his pen to write a description of the pin. One of them drew a picture: it was like a bow. "What would you say its value?" he asked.

"Only sentimental," one said.

The other would have preferred a nominal price. "At least a hundred dollars." She picked a figure out of the air.

He wrote "diamond (?) lover's not," and then appropriately had to go back and insert the "k" to make it, "lover's knot."

If the murderer had wanted that particular jewel, it might account why the bag with the rest of the stuff had been dropped in the hallway. Tully questioned the boy, Johnny Thompson again. He was satisfied that the boy had not seen the diamond pin.

8

As Jimmie drove out to Weston, Connecticut, to be received at court, as he put Mrs. Georgianna Adkins' invitation to dinner, he had already begun to resent the social demands of the case: he was having to give it far too much out-of-office time. Still, he had received the invitation from the old girl herself, and it was quite something to be managing your own affairs even to that detail at the age of eighty-six.

The Adkins mansion was a well-kept relic of another era, probably resembling its owner in that. To be sure, Jimmie could not remember much of those days himself, but his own father had been in the habit of living—when he was at home in Nyack—as though they had never ended. How, Jimmie wondered, had Mrs. Adkins managed through contemporary taxes. Dependency allowances, he decided wryly, remembering that she had three daughters as well as Teddy...three daughters aged, according to *Who's Who,* sixty-five, sixty-four, and sixty-two, and all of them widows. It took a brave man to live in that house. In fact, he decided, squaring his shoulders, it took a brave one to go near it at all.

"I am Miranda Thabor, Mr. Jarvis...Teddy's youngest sister." She came across the marble foyer, her hand extended, and with the movement of a woman of great grace. She was taller than her brother, much more slender, and quite beautiful, even at sixty-two. She waited while Jimmie gave his coat and hat into the hands of the butler, and then led the way through a small waiting parlor. Jimmie opened the great doors for her when they reached them. "We are all home tonight," she said. "Isn't that nice?"

"That's just fine," Jimmie said. He supposed it was.

The grand sitting room was enormous, full of lights and of people. Jimmie saw eight or nine without particularly looking for them. A couple of young men were amongst them, he was glad to observe; all were dressed for dinner and apparently engaged meanwhile each in his own interests, a newspaper, a book, a chess game. Some were even talking.

"Here is Mr. Jarvis, mother," his escort announced him, and everyone then abandoned his own enterprise and followed in Jimmie and Miranda's wake to the old lady's winged chair before the fire.

Jimmie bent low and took the ancient hand in his, a small silken bag of bones. There was no doubting that she was Teddy's mother, her face and eyes were as round as his, and if the ruddy glow was gone from her cheeks a sort of sheen had come into them, yellow but bright.

"It is naughty of Teddy not to be down when his particular guest arrives," she said, giving each word careful guidance around the few teeth left her. Jimmie was amused, remembering that Teddy had used the word "naughty" in speaking of his mother. "I knew your father when he was a young man."

She managed all the introductions herself, each member of the family coming forward as though by signal. "This is my second daughter, Alicia Montelegro, Mr. James Ransom Jarvis...You do use Ransom's name, don't you, Mr. Jarvis?"

"Yes," Jimmie said.

"Alicia," the old lady went on, as though time itself would stand around with the un-introduced members of her family waiting for her to proceed, "married into the Italian House of Clavoy. Do you know they contested the custody of her children and kept the boys in Italy? Very important, it seems..." Jimmie wondered if there were not some oblique promise of her own attitude in the reference. "And we thought they had married us for our money," she concluded the matter and summoned forward another of the family. "This is Theodore Eric Thabor, Miranda's son, named after his uncle, whom he resembles as much as I resemble Cardinal Richelieu."

The resemblance between her and Cardinal Richelieu was not all that remote, Jimmie thought, and glancing down he observed the very glow of mischief in her aged eyes: the old witch had deliberately used the comparison to prompt his consent in it.

She then introduced her oldest daughter who soon after fled to the remotest corner of the room.

"You will promptly forget half the names in our family, Mr. Jarvis, but never mind. It is very unlikely you will find it necessary to speak to most of them again. There are some here I have not spoken to myself for twenty years, I'm sure."

Most of them dispersed then to their own interests within the room.

"Mother Adkins, you don't mind if I run up to the nursery for a minute?" So said one of the granddaughters-in-law whose name Jimmie had already forgot.

"I should certainly prefer it to the nursery's running down here, my dear," the old lady said with a withering dryness. And to Jimmie when the girl was gone, she added matter-of-factly: "I loathe small children, especially female."

Wine was then passed, two kinds of sherry and a very dry madeira which Miranda recommended.

"It deserves your praise," Jimmie said, "I can hear it sing."

Miranda laughed. There was music there, too. Sixty-odd years. My God, but the women in this family preserved themselves and their femininity. And that was something which did not survive if put away in a box. He amused himself with the thought that the basement might be paved with the bones of lovers!

"Have you ever observed the affinity between the Italian

and the English?" Miranda interrupted his reverie. "We are New England, of course, but the pull has reached across to us. When a true New Englander seeks out a warm climate, to this day he goes to Italy."

"Not Florida?"

"Mr. Jarvis, they would rather go to hell than to Palm Beach."

Jimmie accepted another half glass of wine at the moment Teddy Adkins made his entrance, and it occurred to him to wonder if he was thus being repaid for not having been present at his own house when Adkins had first called on him. Teddy was a very neat man. He shook his guest's hand and went then to kiss his mother.

Miranda, whose conversations until then had been adult and not by any means dull, remarked: "Isn't he adorable?" Her eyes upon her brother were worshipful, even when, leaning down to brush his lips to his mother's cheek, he turned his plump little fifty-five-year-old bottom into the air.

Jimmie sipped his wine. He was acutely embarrassed.

"I can very well understand someone's conniving to get him," Miranda said. "But that, as Mama says, is not my affair. It is why you're here though, isn't it, Mr. Jarvis?"

"I am a lawyer," Jimmie said.

"And so very discreet. Don't be distressed. I shall not mention it again."

Somebody had better mention it, Jimmie thought. But very shortly he took Miranda in to dinner while Teddy gave his arm to his mother. She needed no other support.

At the long table over which hung a crystal chandelier, prismatically lustrous as diamonds, twenty people sat down. The butler and two waitresses served them, and the murmur of talk down the table ran to boating, travel, game fishing, and amongst the women someone commented on what an extraordinarily common game tennis had become. Just anybody played it now. All small talk, this, Jimmie thought, reflective of a class, so that it made stand out as the more remarkable, the old lady's sudden statement to Jimmie—a statement for all that it was put as a question: "Did you know, Mr. Jarvis, that I am supported by my son, Theodore?"

"It had not occurred to me to think about it," Jimmie said frankly, but now that he did think about it, he decided she was merely juggling words or perhaps money allotments. Teddy had been very precise in saying that he had not yet come into his inheritance.

"I support the house. He supports me."

Jimmie nodded. The gesture must pass for understanding. He glanced at her plate: a strong mouse could have fetched home such provision.

"For generations it has been the custom in the family, Mr. Jarvis, that the male heir must support his mother as long as she lives before coming himself into nominal possession of the family estate. Perhaps John Wiggam has told you this: he determines each year what he considers a proper share for Theodore to contribute to our household expenses by way of my support in the appropriate fashion. What do you think of the arrangement?"

"It seems to have bred strength to the distaff side, doesn't it?" Jimmie said with a lack of tact quite unusual for him. He didn't really care. It would serve Wiggam right if the Adkins retainer was lost to the firm by the bungling of its junior partner. He had been in no way prepared for this household. "But I assume," he added, having scarcely paused for breath, "it was intended to perpetuate the ideal of individual ruggedness. A tradition beloved of Americans, isn't it?"

Teddy himself turned that to a bad ending: "An ill-served ideal in my case, isn't it?"

"I will not hear you criticize yourself, Teddy," Miranda said. "You have done more splendidly than anyone in this room."

"Just how splendidly we may have yet to learn," Mama said, and then raised her voice to Miranda's son: "Eric, I will not have you shooting in the cove. I have neither time nor patience at this stage of my life to deal with game wardens, and I do not wish to go into the next world answering to bribery in a matter so insignificant."

That, too, was meant for his ears, Jimmie thought. In matters significant she would have no qualms. He learned a good deal by indirection at this otherwise undistinguished meal. In contrast to the service, the fare itself was ordinary. It indicated cookery to the satisfaction of a woman who no longer had any interest in her palate. Jimmie speculated that the cook, too, was a tyrant in her own realm. But he had not come for the food. He found that Teddy almost flinched at the touch of his too-loving sister, Miranda; in fact, when any of his sisters addressed him, he was hard put to raise his eyes to their faces. He had no appreciation of their beauty certainly. What, Jimmie wondered, were his plans for this household when he did come into his inheritance?

As they were about to leave the table, the old lady announced: "You will now excuse Mr. Jarvis and myself. He and I will take our coffee upstairs."

On his arm, she piloted the way to the elevator. The butler hastened after them and took them up. The fire had been lit in her sitting room.

"Well, Mr. Jarvis," she said, to the point immediately: "what do you think of Miss Daisy Thayer?"

"I think she has a fair case against your son," Jimmie said.

"Good. I'm delighted to hear that. She will not be tempted to drop it. Do you suppose they lived together as she claims? Be frank with me, young man."

"I think you should ask your son to be frank with you, Mrs. Adkins."

"I have a very good reason for not asking him. He has not been reared to be frank about such things with his mother. She may win then?"

Jimmie realized that was exactly how the old lady wanted it.

"Let me put it this way," Jimmie said. "Her chances are sufficiently good that I would recommend a reasonable settlement out of court."

"Nonsense!" the old woman cried. "I will not hear of it. Shame on Teddy for putting you up to it. Why, that would settle nothing."

"Am I right that no matter which way the court settles, you will be satisfied?"

"If we lose, we win," she said. "You understand me thoroughly, Mr. Jarvis. I do not wish to raise someone else's bastard, but I'd rather have one of Teddy's than no child at all."

"I was thinking of the family," Jimmie said. "There's bound to be publicity. I don't suppose you would try to persuade your son to marry the woman?"

"I have very little inclination that way. Besides which, it would not settle anything either. I want you to fight this thing, Mr. Jarvis. I want you to use all your skill toward winning. No quarter, no mercy, no shame. You understand that?"

"It is the only way I can serve both you and your son," Jimmie said, "whatever your separate motives."

To lose a hard-fought battle in the court, Jimmie thought, would strengthen the child's authenticity: this, he took to be the driving force behind old Mrs. Adkins. There was small purpose to trying to explain to her the fallibility of juries in such cases.

"As you pointed out, Mr. Jarvis, there will be publicity. I am prepared for it, however it distresses my poor boy. I am sure it will not distress Miss Daisy Thayer. It may even bring her one of those seals of approval by which Hollywood certifies the genuineness of a woman. Have you seen her?"

"No, I haven't."

"I don't mean talked to her. I mean viewed her, cased her, whatever that word is which police use."

"I know what you mean," Jimmie said.

"How do you know what she'll look like before a jury?"

"I've not got that far, Mrs. Adkins. As a matter of fact, I am at the moment casing you."

The old lady liked that. She nodded approval. "You need more than one evening for that, young man. I've had a look at her myself, you know. A perfume counter is in the public domain." She sighed then. "I should not be surprised if Miss Thayer is also. Well. You may go now, Mr. Jarvis. I shall expect to see you again soon."

As soon as he had left her Jimmie realized he had managed no stronger persuasion with her than had Teddy. He shuddered to think what a lifetime in this household could do to any man.

9

At nine-thirty the next morning Jimmie was waiting outside his office door for Mr. Wiggam. The senior partner was not especially pleased to start his day with the Adkins affair, but Jimmie cared not: he was starting and ending his with it.

"You see, sir, Teddy wants to settle out of court. His mother seems to think it would be better to fight it through the courts. But the peculiar twist to this thing is, sir: Teddy maintains his innocence. His mother rather hopes he will come out guilty."

"Nonsense," Wiggam said.

"No sir. I spent the evening with her. Very simply, she would like a grandson in or out of wedlock. And if the court says Teddy's the father, she would be willing to take that word over his."

"Well, Jim," Wiggam said after a long moment's thought, "we're Georgianna's lawyers. If he hoped to settle it quietly, young Teddy should have got himself an attorney. Curious he didn't, isn't it when you stop to think about the situation? Why did he tell Georgianna at all?"

"Miss Thayer wants a hundred thousand dollars," Jimmie said. "Adkins doesn't have it. I suspect he misjudged his mother—thinking she would come across. By the way, how much does he contribute to his mother's support, Mr. Wiggam?"

"Five thousand this year. I set the figure myself."

"So I was given to understand. Having been a guest in the house, I'd be curious to know how you arrived at the figure, sir."

"Very simple. I took the expenditures of the previous year, and divided the amount by the average number of people living within the family household. Primitive arithmetic."

Jimmie agreed. Twenty people had sat down to dinner. To reverse Wiggam's mathematics, multiply five thousand by twenty. Sufficient to run the average house! "Isn't 'primary' arithmetic the word, Mr. Wiggam?"

Mr. Wiggam made one of his rare excursions into humor. "When I do it, it's primitive."

Jimmie smiled. "Is he a good business man, Adkins?"

"I suspect he's no more than adequate," Wiggam said. "We let him in on the administration of the estate a few years ago. It was an unhappy event. My own suspicion is he earns only what he needs. And I don't suppose there's anything wrong with that."

"It's rather admirable if it works," Jimmie said.

Wiggam said nothing. It was not his notion of enterprise.

"Did you know Adkins as a young man, sir?"

"I've been trying to think of my earliest recollection of him," Wiggam said. "I think it rather typical: he was in swaddles. The nurse had left him for a moment in charge of his sisters. They were in a perfect fury over him, poor lad, pulling him, one from the other, and he screaming. . ."

"Perhaps you remember him to better advantage later," Jimmie suggested.

"I'm afraid I remember the same sort of squabble on an adult level next," Mr. Wiggam said. "When it came time for him to go to college the girls came home from the ends of the earth in order to have something to say about it. Very dominating women in that family. In the end, Georgianna, his mother, put that up to me also. It was very simple, really. His father was a Harvard man. What better solution than send the boy there?"

"Do you know, sir, this is the first time I have heard the father mentioned?"

Wiggam sat in a moment's silent contemplation at the end of which he said: "Poor old Ted. I'd forgot him myself. Very quiet man. He died just after Teddy was born."

Jimmie was tempted to ask if it was in childbirth, but he said nothing. He doubted Wiggam would be amused.

"I don't suppose I've seen Teddy a half-dozen times since, all told, certainly not to talk to," he summarized with dwindling patience. "Somebody must know him."

Jimmie knew he had been dismissed. No doubt somebody did know, he thought, and he wanted to know him better himself, considerably better before going into court to defend his honor. He went back to *Who's Who*. The information on Teddy was meager, but at least it indicated Harvard, 1924, and membership then in the "Skiddoo" Club.

He sat back and thought over his acquaintanceship among Harvard alumni. Finally by the intermediation of a mutual friend, he was in touch with a Skiddoo man of the class of '24.

10

Jimmie met Martin Rider at the Harvard Club in late afternoon. It was not until they found a picture in the 1924 class publications that Rider could place Theodore E. Adkins. Jimmie thought the face of his client, by that picture, oddly unchanged in over thirty years. A curious thing about Rider: while he could not remember Teddy, he recognized the family name immediately. "They're the Tripp Gold Mines people."

It conjured a strange picture for Jimmie: little round Teddy sitting by a water's edge, panning gold. He mentioned it to his companion.

Rider laughed. "It's a long year past since that family did any of their own panning. But now, you know, you've almost brought Adkins back to me, the sense, the feeling, an intimacy of him. What the devil is it now. . .?"

He went over the Skiddoo Club book and suddenly he leaned back. "Oh, my God, sure. I remember him now. You know how it is with fellows that age—boasting about the women in their lives? And that was the twenties. Well, little Teddy Adkins used to turn up at our bull sessions with the most fantastic stories of his conquests. And no matter how we bated him, he stuck by his stories.

"So, of course, kindness not being especially characteristic of boys that age, we set a trap. A couple of the fellows followed him on one of his twilight excursions. They followed him to the edge of the river—a place well off the road—but there he took off every stitch of his clothes and sat down. Naked, with his arms and legs folded, he sat for a solid hour like a bare Buddha. Then he got up, dressed, walked into town, stopped at a soda fountain and had a Green River, and then came back to the dorm. The spies got home about ten minutes ahead of him and we were waiting for him. But he came in and looked around.

"'Gentlemen,' he said, and I can see him to this day, apple cheeks, a tuft of blond hair. . . 'I regret to say I have nothing to report tonight. I have been stood up. One hour I waited at our usual rendezvous, and made a feast, alas, only for the mosquitoes. Oh, the perfidy of woman!' He always did have an old-fashioned way of talking. And you see, we'd had the rug pulled out from under us. Or maybe it was our leg, both legs. I'll tell you this, Jarvis. We left him alone after that."

"You believed him?" said Jimmie.

"Let's put it this way, we respected him, and even if we didn't admit it, we were probably a little scared of him. Looking back on it all now, I'd be inclined to say he was as canny as he was imaginative. He probably knew he was being followed. He put the only silencer possible on us. Like Lot's wife, we were stricken dumb. But think of the nerve it took to do that, man."

Jimmie nodded. But it was not the sort of tale one told a jury by way of assuring them of a man's innocence. And it did seem a bit thick that one who started life so cannily should fall easy victim to the scheme of Miss Thayer. Still, the episode showed a ken of the ways of men, not of the wiles of women.

"Any other recollections of our friend?" he asked.

"He had a flare for dramatics," Rider said.

"Redundant," said Jimmie.

"I remember his habit of getting sick on every visitors' day. He could even manage a temperature."

"At the merest thought of his sisters, no doubt," Jimmie said.

"That's right!" Rider cried. "We used to call them—what's the play with the three sisters in it?"

"The Cherry Orchard," Jimmie suggested.

"No. Shakespeare, *King Lear.*"

"Goneril, Regan and Cordelia," Jimmie recalled.

"I remember one of his papers in English Lit about them. He could be very amusing. He undertook to prove the young one—the one that's supposed to be the old man's angel child—Teddy set out to prove her the arch villainess of literature. It was her sickening sweetness that made a weakling of the old man. Otherwise there wouldn't have been a play. That was his thesis. You might be able to find that. Do you mind my asking—are you writing a book about him? I know—you're ghosting his autobiography."

Jimmie grinned. "Not quite."

His companion shrugged. "Most everybody who can afford it is having it done these days. Maybe it's cheaper than psychoanalysis at that."

Jimmie got up. "Let me buy you a drink," he said. "No. It will be in the papers soon I expect. He's the defendant in a paternity suit."

"Little Teddy Adkins? Well, I'll be damned."

"Just what is it that surprises you?"

"Why, that he got caught, man. He's smarter than that."

"That's just fine," Jimmie said.

He decided to walk home to see if he could pace some order into his mind. It began to look as though there were at least two faces to Theodore Adkins, and juries were not notoriously partial to two-faced defendants.

11

Mrs. Norris powdered her nose and shook a few drops of lavender on a handkerchief which she tucked into her bosom. In an association she had clung to for well over fifty years, she could remember her mother calling her "her wild Annie" and pulling her head into her bosom a minute before taking the comb to the snarls in her hair. The smell of lavender had been as deep in her mother's breast as though it were grown there.

She was putting on her tea apron when the doorman phoned up and said that Mr. Adkins was in the elevator. "But Mr. James is not home," she said, without thinking to whom she said it.

"Is it a chaperon you want? I'll come up myself when I go off duty in a few minutes."

"Just polish your brass buttons, young man," Mrs. Norris said.

The doorman, who had managed to slip past retirement age without calling attention to it, tittered.

Mrs. Norris hung up the phone in disgust. A couple of moments later she opened the door to a smiling Mr. Adkins. He stood, his hat in hand and a portfolio under his arm. "I promised Mr. Jarvis some papers at my earliest convenience. I hope it's at his—or yours—to admit me now, Mrs. Norris?"

"Mr. James is not at home, but I expect he will be before long. It is after five, isn't it?"

Adkins consulted a gold watch which he took from his vest pocket. "Five twenty-seven. I rather assumed he would leave his office at five."

He gave his portfolio into Mrs. Norris' hands and took off his topcoat. She had no choice but to put him and his portfolio in a chair. After all he was a client, and an affable man. But neither she nor her master liked to be called upon without advance notice, and Mr. James had not mentioned his coming. She lighted a lamp and then took a match to the fire set in the grate. Mr. Adkins bounced to her side, and saved her the stoop before she was well into it. In fact they were both suspended for a few seconds halfway between a squat and a stance, face to face. Mr. Adkins lifted his nose and fairly rolled it up in a sniff.

"Heather!" he cried. "Or is it lavender?"

"Lavender," Mrs. Norris said, but the word "heather" had scored with her nonetheless, and she remembered his having told her he had been in Scotland as a boy. Or had he been transported only by the tales of a Scottish nurse?

He put the match to the paper and kindling, and then stood back, turning his hands about before the sudden flames; his eyes seemed absolutely sky blue, and sparkled with the firelight. "I have been thinking of Scotland—and of you, Mrs. Norris—since last we met. You've not been back for a long time, have you?"

"Not for many a long year, though I got my passport a while back thinking I'd go soon."

"Don't go alone," he said very solemnly. "It will mark the end of youth if you do."

"I took that turn in the path several bends ago, Mr. Adkins."

"No. Not as long as you can find your way back, ever," he said, and flashed her a smile of persuasion. "Age is something sudden and absolute. Age is getting lost. And that's why I said not to return to Scotland alone. To arrive and not find there the welcome which you had conjured..."

"Then all I'd have to do is turn around and come back. The ground is solid enough under my feet in America," she said.

Mr. Adkins laughed. "Well said!"

He could say things well himself, she thought. She liked the bit: age was getting lost. One of the things she liked best about a man was a good manner of speaking. Likely the reason she had never got married again, the Jarvis men had spoiled her with their talk; she could not abide the thought of a man coming home at the end of the day with his head as empty as his dinner bucket; and they were the kind available. But Annie

Norris was not by any means available to them.

"Stay a moment and talk with me," Mr. Adkins said disarmingly. "Do you know a book called *Ballads of the North Countrie?*"

"I know you spell countree with an 'i' and an 'e'," she said.

"That's the one. I used to know half the book by rote. I fancied myself a balladeer. I thought it would win me someone fair, my quavering tenor, or someone congenial. No one who likes a song lacks congeniality, Mrs. Norris."

"That's true," she said, and then amended it: "depending of course, on what you call a song. There are things they call songs today a cat wouldn't throw a shoe at."

It took a few minutes, but Mrs. Norris was presently, and without her quite knowing how it came about, persuaded at least to the edge of a cane-bottomed chair, to talk to him. A nice thing about the man was his way of drawing out the best things she had to say and in a way which made her pleased with herself for having said them. Their talk came round to the uses America had made of the old country songs—in the mountains, the coal mines, on the railways, which naturally enough, the railways having been strung across the country on Irish melodies, turned her thoughts to Mr. Tully. She found herself telling Mr. Adkins about her friend, the detective.

Mr. Adkins showed his beautiful teeth in a gleam of satisfaction. It was too bad he didn't have as many hairs on his head as teeth inside it.

"What kind of detection does he do?" Mr. Adkins asked.

"All kinds," she said, "all the important kinds. He's the

chief investigator for the district attorney. Right now it's murder, and an important one it must be. I've not seen him, face or fancy, since the night they found the woman."

"Has it been in the newspapers?" said Adkins, apparently intrigued.

"Of course it has, though in moderation. Mr. Tully is a man of moderation. It was the woman up near Harlem—Mrs. Arabella Sperling. Isn't that a lovely name to be done in with?"

Mr. Adkins seemed shocked, and Mrs. Norris realized she had come to take murder with the lack of personal involvement a policeman had to have.

"I didn't mean that quite the way it came out, Mr. Adkins," she explained. "But we cannot grieve at everyone else's tragedy. We'd have no strength at all when it came to our own if we did."

"Oh," the little man cried, "I agree, I quite agree. Is there a mystery about it? I love a good mystery."

"You'd better follow it in the papers then," Mrs. Norris said. "It has all the promise of turning out to be that."

"Then they don't know who killed her?"

"The last I heard there was no arrest," she said. For all she was hearing these days from Jasper Tully, the criminal could be in the Tombs now, waiting trial. "But, of course, my friend doesn't tell me everything."

"And I dare say you don't repeat everything he does tell you," Adkins prompted. "You seem to be a woman of rare discretion."

The clock was striking six. "I must get some ice. Mr. James

will want to make drinks for you and himself." She was suddenly feeling the need of a pickup herself. Was it mention of Tully? He was getting along without her very well these days, as the song said. And Annie Norris was not a woman to delude herself. She was not one who would live on fancy, trailing her dreams like a tattered petticoat when the truth failed her. She got up and gave her shoulders a rustle as though to test the starch in them.

Mr. Adkins, watching her, did not get up because he knew it would offend her sense of fitness, and they had got on very nicely that afternoon. When she reached the door, he said:

"Next time I come here, I shall bring you my copy of *The North Countrie* if you would like to read again some of the old ballads."

"I'd be honored, sir," she said, and gave a little bob of a curtsey that she had always found the best way to get out of a room when you were torn between going and staying.

It was too much for Mr. Adkins, fitness or no. He leapt to his feet and bowed low.

12

Jimmie, having spent the greater part of that day as well as the two preceding evenings either with the person or the problems of Teddy Adkins, could have thought of several people he would have preferred to find waiting in his study.

"You asked me to bring you these newspaper bits as soon as I could," Adkins said. "Otherwise I should not be here. I'm sure you are already approaching satiety with myself and my family."

"Not at all," Jimmie murmured and fortified himself with a stiff drink. Teddy took sherry.

"We should not have this grab-bag of my adventures and misadventures if it weren't for the dotage of my sisters. But we do have it. So we may as well use it if it turns me out a gentleman." He opened the portfolio and took a neat scrap book of clippings from it. "How would you like to have had your life catalogued from mewl to middle-age by three doting sisters?"

"It would drive me to a double life," Jimmie said, hoping to start a gleam of appreciation in Adkins' eye.

He did not even look up. "Is there anyone in this world who lives but a single life?"

"Let's see what you've got here," Jimmie said, and pulled up two chairs to the large library table.

Teddy opened the book. The caption on the first piece of yellowed newspaper read: *Sit Down Strikers in Brooklyn Encouraged by Socialite.*

Adkins ran a long delicate finger along the words and then pointed to the picture of a man, his back to the camera, his fist in the air, apparently addressing a windowful of factory workers.

"That is I," he said proudly.

"What?" said Jimmie.

"Oh, yes. My sympathies have always been with the people outside. Certainly you did not think me at home in the bosom of my family?"

Jimmie took a long pull at his drink. "It did occur to me to wonder what you would do with that menage when you came into your inheritance."

"I shall put a match to the house in the dead of night, set up an alarum, and watch them run out in their nightclothes. It will be interesting to see how they go about living when there is nothing left for them to eat but one another."

He said it with such calmness, detachment, that a shiver ran through Jimmie, his reaction compounded of both horror and delight. He turned to another page of the album. The clipping there was of a May Day parade in New York City, headed: *The Commies' Thinning Ranks.*

"There I am," Teddy said. "Bold and balder."

"This is great," Jimmie said. He was going into court to defend a Red in a paternity suit. "A Communist's word is not gospel to most Americans, you know, and their behavior in court hasn't endeared them to judge or jury."

"But my dear boy, I am not a Communist. I loathe them. That's why I'm there. They should not have a monopoly on the defense of men's rights. And I certainly didn't want to surrender the first of May to them. Though why I should cherish it, I don't know. One of the most dreadful of my childhood recollections is of prancing around a maypole with my shoes full of gravel."

Jimmie scratched his head. "I suppose there's a sort of logic to your reasoning. I'm not sure Mr. Wiggam is going to see it."

"My dear Jarvis, if my mother saw it, Wiggam will see it. He will have to."

"Quite true," said Jimmie. On the whole he was not displeased with this new picture of little Teddy Adkins which was emerging. He was showing up to be a man of good will, however dubious seemed his wisdom. . .or was he merely an exhibitionist? "Wouldn't you like to leave the album with me for a day or two? I won't use any information without your consent."

"I doubt I shall be more uncomfortable at your using it than at your culling it." Adkins wiped the perspiration from his hands on a handkerchief. "It is rather embarrassing, you know."

Jimmie grinned. "You must think of me as you would a psychiatrist, Mr. Adkins."

"Do you know, I've often thought I'd go to one, but I'm afraid it would spoil the fun I get out of life." Adkins finished his sherry. "I don't like to leave that about really," he said, referring again to the scrap book.

"I'll go over it right away," Jimmie said, and took him to the door himself.

Finally, just before the door closed on him, Adkins said: "Don't leave it where your housekeeper will find it, will you?"

"I'll lock it up," said Jimmie, "although I'd leave my own diary with Mrs. Norris."

"But you lead such an exemplary life," Mr. Adkins said. He flashed his transitory smile and departed.

What the hell does he know about my exemplary life, Jimmie thought, returning to his study. It was particularly irksome to have heard the man say it because it was all too true. He poured a drink and took it to Mrs. Norris' sitting room off the kitchen. She would not help herself to one unless she was about to go into a faint.

She looked up from the afternoon paper. "Ah, Mister Jamie, thank you. He's gone, is he?"

"For the present. I don't very much like his habit of popping in. I hope it doesn't annoy you."

"If it took no more than that to annoy me, you could put me out to pasture. I find him a congenial man." She saw that Jimmie was reading her paper. "You may have it if you like, sir."

"Excuse me," Jimmie said, and stated what he had come in about: "Could you give me something to eat on a cracker? Where I'm going tonight we won't sit down to dinner till nine."

"There's not one word about Mr. Tully's case in the whole paper. It's all about those dreadful boys going around in gangs..."

Jimmie eased himself out of a discussion of them, and realized even as he was doing it that too many people in New York were doing the same thing.

In his study again, he was about to put Adkins' scrap book away for the night when another item in it attracted his attention. It was from a morning New York paper of a year and a half before: *Minister Exonerated in Murder of Girl.*

Jimmie but vaguely remembered the affair as he read the lead paragraph. The case had been dismissed. He had been in Washington, himself, but if nothing else came back to him about the trial, the name of the victim did: Ellie True. He had thought then, as likely did anyone who could carry a tune, that someone should write a ballad on *The Murder of Ellie True.*

Jimmie put down the album, deliberately stopping his

eyes from racing through the article. He was in the habit of plucking meat and marrow from the newspaper, leaving the bones to be picked by those who read nothing else. But he had one of those rare premonitions of something in this for the connoisseur. He mixed himself another drink and took it to the window to mull with his speculation. The sky beyond the flickering mountains of buildings to the south of the park was a deep blue flecked with stars high up, but pearly at the buildings' rim. Clear, exquisitely clear, as the lives of men most certainly were not, Jimmie mused paraphrasing a poem which was not exquisitely clear to him either.

What in the murder of Ellie True had interested Teddy Adkins? Whatever it was that had led to the dismissal of charges against the man accused of her murder, he speculated. He returned to the piece. He had been quite right:

"The break came in the twelfth day of the dramatic trial of the Reverend Alfonzo Blake. Defense Counsel Elmo Mumford introduced the witness who corroborated Dr. Blake's alibi for the night of the murder. Defense counsel then motioned for the dismissal of the trial. Judge Wilkins adjourned court for ten minutes. Returning from his chambers, he dismissed the charges and discharged the jury.

"The real drama of the case developed quietly in the search by wealthy socialite Theodore E. Adkins for the 'so-called' missing witness. Adkins became interested in the case when convinced by newspaper accounts that Dr. Blake was telling the truth. Reached at his Connecticut home, Mr. Adkins said:

'I am deeply gratified. I am sure Dr. Blake has many years of provident ministry before him.'"

Provident ministry, Jimmie thought: the peculiar combination of words was characteristic of Teddy Adkins. He made a note to himself. He knew the attorney, Elmo Mumford, a noted trial lawyer, and he intended to see him at the first opportunity.

13

Mrs. Norris had found nothing in the newspaper about Arabella Sperling's murder, because nothing new had been turned up, nothing at least that Jasper Tully was willing to give the newspapers.

The Medical Examiner's report was filed. It showed that nothing out of the ordinary was likely to have occurred to Mrs. Sperling the day of her death, nothing strange in the way of food or drink, or physical activity. If she had gone to bed with a gentleman that night—and by the evidence obtained so far it was thoroughly improper to suggest it—it had been in the strictly literal sense, to sleep at his side.

Only Oscar Johanson dared suggest the existence of such a man. And he had had reason to hope profoundly that one existed. No one except Jasper Tully believed him. But miraculously for both of them, his innocence was attested by the report of the Medical Examiner: two lovely tapering thumbs, almost feminine—and perhaps they were—in their delicacy, had stopped the flow of breath through Mrs. Sperling's throat.

Johanson held up his thumbs on Lieutenant Greer's command.

"As dainty as barnacles," Greer said in deep disgust. "Get the hell out of here and you don't have to come back."

"That only means you're no longer his number one suspect," Tully said, walking out of the interview room with him. "We may need you one of these days to do some identifying. So don't go far from home." He waited until the man was a few steps on his way, a new man, and then called: "Johanson...I wonder if you'd mind giving me a description again of the man you saw leaving her house that morning? It won't take long."

"Sure," Johanson said.

Afterwards Tully made up his more mundane description from Johanson's reaccounting of what his Jim-dandy walking doll looked like. It read:

Height: not more than 5' 8", probably 5' 6"
Weight: 160-170
Build: stocky
Complexion: Ruddy. "Like well-fed Englishman"
Hair: Uncertain. Blond probably. (possibly bald.)
Mustache: English type. Blond, curly (Edwardian?)

Glasses: Dark-rimmed. (which he took off to better see Sperling in window. Probably frequent gesture as common to people who see distances better without glasses)
Clothes: Light gray hat, gray (herringbone?) topcoat. Dark suit. Carried black umbrella rolled up. (Brief case?)
Peculiarities: Manner of walking, back on heels. Vital, lively step. (Of man of well being?) Very neat in appearance.

Tully drove Johanson home himself. He went then to the funeral parlor from which Mrs. Sperling had been buried and picked up the names of those who had called to pay condolences and had signed "the book of sympathy." There was not such a number of them and Tully resolved to see each of them himself. He might then come out with a picture of the victim.

He expected to see a fairly complete roster of the deceased's friends. Very few people made such calls without leaving a mark to show they had been there, even if a scented book of sympathy turned their stomachs. Within a couple of hours the witnesses began to appear at the District Attorney's office in response to Tully's calls.

The first man he saw was Jefferson Tope, the minister who had given the message of departure, to put it in his words.

"She was not always what I should call a church woman," the Reverend Tope said. His parish church was on Lexington Avenue, a few blocks south of where Mrs. Sperling had lived. "But I've been wondering if there was not a kind of pattern in her attendance. For example, she had not been to church since August eleventh. I looked it up in her contribution record. A fairly generous woman. I mentioned that to the nieces at the funeral, by the way. They seemed to disagree, but then I should scarcely credit their views in such matters."

Tully could guess why: it would have fallen to the nieces to contribute to his ministry after the funeral. No doubt it was a meager benefice, and likely squabbled over in his presence.

"Mrs. Sperling's church attendance," the detective said. "How long had she been going regular before September?"

"Very nearly a year. But there's the pattern part. . .some time in her rather spotty attendance before last year, she came to me and asked me what I would think of her marrying a divorced man. She was not really a very attractive woman, Mr. Tully, if I may be pardoned for speaking frankly of the dead. I mentioned that she was generous. I must temper that now to say that my own impression of her generosity was that she intended to buy something with every cent she gave, and I wonder now if she didn't buy. . .friendship."

Tully could not help but observe the cleric's thumbs. He supposed that until this case was closed he would examine the thumbs of every human being he encountered. The Reverend's ran to curls. They resembled two question marks.

"What about the divorced man?" the detective asked.

"Well, you see, my first question to her was: does he have a family to support? 'He does,' she said. 'I would help him.' But I don't think anything came of their romance. Very soon she was back at church as regular as Sunday."

"Did she mentioned the name of the man?"

"No. I suggested that she bring him to see me. She promised that she would. Naturally I didn't mention it when she didn't."

"I'm not sure I see the pattern," Tully said.

"Mrs. Sperling's whole attendance has been a series of devout periods and lax periods."

"Do you think she came in to pray for a husband between prospects, Mr. Tope?"

"I shouldn't be that precise about it," the minister said, "but I do think she returned to God in periods of loneliness."

"Most of us do if we're going to turn at all," Tully said.

One thing that had come from the Reverend Tope's testimony, he thought when the man was gone, was that the picture the two nieces tried to give of their aunt—her being a woman who would not have a man cross her threshold—was entirely inaccurate.

Another payer of last respects to Mrs. Sperling turned out to be a representative of her bank, an honest mourner no doubt, Tully thought. Appropriately, it was the lad through whom she had made her last withdrawal. Tully asked if she had seemed nervous, taking out so large a sum of money.

"I told Lieutenant Greer she seemed nervous, sir, but the more I think of it, it wasn't a worried kind of nervousness. I mean—well, she giggled once or twice."

Somehow Tully would never have thought Arabella Sperling to have giggled in her whole life. "But she didn't make any excuses, any explanation for wanting five thousand dollars in small bills?"

"Oh, yes she did, sir. I went to the cashier for an okay when she wanted that much money, you see. We should have more notice. And she told him in my presence it was for a real estate investment. He looked at her in a way—I suppose you'd call it questioning. After all, in small bills. And she said, 'My broker recommends it,' and then gave that silly smile of hers you had to be watching to see. The cashier made her say it over again: 'Your broker, Mrs. Sperling?' 'MY broker.' And when she said it that way, that was that."

Tully thanked him and thought about his information. It contradicted Johanson's, though the building superintendent might not necessarily be lying about it. The bank teller quoted Mrs. Sperling as saying her "broker" recommended the cash real estate deal, whereas Johanson quoted her as saying her "broker" had turned it down. The one thing the detective was quite sure about now, Johanson did not get the money; the murderer did. If he had engineered the withdrawal of five thousand dollars, it proved premeditation: murder without passion. And everything about the house, its neatness, confirmed that.

Another signer of the sympathy book arrived, and another. . .several who contributed nothing to the investigation.

Then came George Allan Masters, a man visibly uneasy at the prospect of an interview with the District Attorney's representative. He gave his age as fifty-one, his occupation, shoe salesman. In response to the routine question on his marital status, he said with hesitancy, "Ah—married."

Tully thought he knew who he was. "Recently, Mr. Masters?"

"Yes, sir. My second marriage, that is."

"Widowed or divorced?"

"Divorced."

"Children?"

"Three—by my first marriage. The oldest is sixteen."

"Between the hours of six and midnight of Friday, November 17, where were you?"

"Last Friday," the man said slowly, and then hastily: "That isn't difficult: I was in the store, except between six and seven, when I went out with my boss for supper. We took inventory that night. Finished up about two in the morning."

Tully was glad to get that one out of the way himself. "Thank you."

"Is that the time Arabella was killed?"

"Sometime before midnight," Tully said. "At one time you and Mrs. Sperling were considering marriage, weren't you?"

Masters looked startled but not frightened. "I didn't know anyone knew that except Arabella herself. Yes, sir, we were."

"What happened to it, your plan?"

"Well, I was a good deal fonder of my present wife. To tell you the God's truth, sir, I wasn't fond of Arabella at all, and in the end I couldn't be a hypocrite."

"How's that?"

"Arabella offered to help out with the children—in a financial way—if I married her. It was tempting. I don't make enough money to support two households. I didn't want to come here today in case you'd speak to my boss and jeopardize my job..."

"I'm always careful not to get anybody into trouble who doesn't deserve it," Tully said. "I want to know about Mrs. Sperling, and you can tell me more than most people. You knew her well enough to talk about marriage…"

"She saw to that and often enough," the man interjected.

"And yet you weren't very fond of her. Didn't you like her even at first?"

"Oh, yes. She could be nice. And she seemed awfully generous. But I'll try to tell you how it got to be: well, the only way I can say it—when she'd give you something, she'd snatch it back, and maybe your arm, too. She had that awful way of getting hold of you. Not with her hands. It was just her way, her personality."

Tully thought he understood. The same picture had come through from the Reverend Tope. It was an ungentle irony that someone had in the end got hold of Arabella—by the throat. This lad had thumbs like clothes pins, and fingernails he might use for shoehorns. He could not have grown them since the murder, and such nails would have marked the skin of the victim.

"You aren't the first person to feel that way about Arabella Sperling," the detective said.

"I'm glad of that," Masters said quietly. "We don't always see straight, trying to look round our own problems."

"She did want to get married, didn't she?" Tully mused.

"She sure did."

"You wouldn't think it'd be so hard, her having money. Where did you meet her?"

"Three years or so ago—at a place called the Mellody Friendship Club. It's on Twenty-second Street, near Third Avenue."

There was something rang a bell with Tully about the Mellody Friendship Club. But the harder he thought about it, the more unfamiliar it grew. He was probably reminded of something he had seen on television, he decided, for a play did begin to come back to him—a murder outside the door while all these nice, gentle people were inside dancing at arms' length from each other.

"That's where people go with the object of meeting somebody marriageable, isn't it?" he said.

"I'd put it this way—I don't think anybody who's happily married would see much point in going there. And Mrs. Mellody wouldn't have anybody there who was unhappily married. Not if she knew it."

"They're trouble, are they?" said Tully. "She wants you lonesome but not miserable."

Masters ventured a smile. "That's about it."

"Now I'm a widower. I've got a good job—at least most kids between six and sixteen would like to grow up in it, so I guess it's a good job—and I'm getting to the lonesome age. Do you suppose it's the place for me?"

"I'd recommend it very highly," Masters said with the smugness of one who no longer needed its hospitality.

"I guess I'll go see Mrs. Mellody at that," Tully said.

14

Anyone who frequented the Criminal Court building as regularly as did Jimmie was bound to run into Elmo Mumford, and this time Jimmie did it deliberately. Mumford was a member of that rare and distinguished breed: the trial lawyer. He had a head on him like Daniel Webster in both size and content, and he bore it with the air of one aggrieved it had not yet been sculpted by an artist worthy of the subject.

Now Jimmie had a very good friend who was a sculptor, or to be precise, a sculptress, of considerable reputation. She was spending a year in England, but Mumford didn't know her to be out of the country. Not only did he shake Jimmie's hand on their meeting; he threw his arm about his shoulder, and avowed they must have lunch together.

"Are you free today?" said Jimmie.

"Happens I am," Mumford cried. "How's Helene? It must be a year since I've seen her. She wanted to do me, you know. You wouldn't mind, would you, old man?" He gave Jimmie an elbow in the ribs, then steered him out of the building and down the street two blocks to his own favorite restaurant. Jimmie wondered if the imperious manner made him a better lawyer. It certainly made him seem one.

But he was a good conversationalist and he treated Jimmie as a patron of the arts. It was quite pleasant in fact, and he allowed Jimmie to choose their wine, a compliment he avowed, which his palate allowed him to pay but rarely. It was with some reluctance that Jimmie steered their conversation around to the murder of Ellie True.

"Oh, by the Almighty, what a mincemeat we made of your old office in that one!" Mumford shook with pleasure at the recollection.

Jimmie assumed he meant the District Attorney's office. With something understandably close to self-pity, he felt great sympathy for the prosecutor of the Reverend Alfonzo Blake. It was bad enough to have the case dismissed, but the bad publicity connected with having brought insupportable charges against a man of God. . .enough to stunt the ambition even of a district attorney. "Who tried that one for the Office?" Jimmie asked.

Mumford mentioned the Assistant District Attorney.

"It wasn't old Jasper Tully who did the ground work for him, was it?"

"No. We didn't get the top boys. I'll say that for them. Tully and his boss were tied up in a Labor Rackets hearing at Federal Court."

Jimmie felt much better. He was not a man who thrived on another's mismanagements. And that was why he was not likely ever to be a trial lawyer of Mumford's calibre: he lacked the deadly sense of competition. "Maybe you were lucky then," he said.

"I might have been at that," Mumford admitted with surprising humility. "Ever come across a queer little duck called Theodore E. Adkins?"

"Yes," Jimmie said.

"Yes, what?"

Jimmie drew a deep breath. Nobody ever got anything for nothing from Elmo Mumford. "I'm about to defend him in a paternity suit."

"Now that's a twist! By the Almighty, that is a twist. Who is it that finally got the knife into the poor bastard? He's been a sitting duck for years."

"I think I'd rather let her get her own publicity," Jimmie said. "What do you know about Adkins?"

"He's a born meddler. Not a do-gooder, mind you. He's a calculator, and I wouldn't underestimate his intelligence for a minute. If she's got the knife in deep enough, though, I'd try to get her to take it out without twisting. Pay off a little. I'll tell you why. If you put him on the stand in something like this, he won't do himself any good. Too much ego. He's got to show how clever he is. You can't be clever out of one side of your mouth and naive out of the other. And naïveté is the only winning defense I know in these things." Mumford brushed crumbs from the table. "But he couldn't play it that way. Messy business. Old family, too. Settle out of court. That's my advice. Which, come to think of it, you didn't ask, did you?"

"I might have," Jimmie said, "if I could take it. But we shall go to law, and for a variety of complex reasons. The best I can do for myself right now is find out what I can about the man I'm defending. How did Adkins come into the Ellie True affair?"

Mumford thought for a moment and then snorted: "Damned if I know how he came in. The way I came to try the case myself was irregular. I was asked to take it by a fraternal organization I belong to. I don't like getting these holy men. I don't understand them, and if you can't pull them out clean as a baby's tooth, you might as well let go of them. There's no such thing with juries as mitigating circumstances for fallen angels. Now I have not lost a man to the chair yet." He rapped heavy knuckles on the table. "And by the Almighty, I didn't want to do it for charity!"

Mumford sat back in his chair, refused a cigarette, accepted a cigar. "I wonder where Reverend Blake is now. Texas would be my guess—the land of opportunity. Tell you something, Jimmie—I don't have any more faith in him today than I had on our first interview. Did he kill her?" Mumford shrugged. "He was the self-appointed pastor of something called the Mellody Friendship Club, one of those homey places where misfits and myopics can sit and hold hands. Ellie True was a waitress at the club. Not a customer. That was how things came to look very bad for the Reverend Blake in the first place.

"The night Ellie was murdered, he admitted having called on her—as well as every member of the club—to deliver some salvation literature. A witness saw him in her apartment—and one of the few things in his favor at that stage, was that the witness had been able to see him because he and Ellie had left the door open—but no one saw him close the door or leave the apartment. That was about ten o'clock. It makes a long day even for a minister.

"When Ellie's room-mate came home at two A.M. she found Ellie in bed—suffocated to death, probably by a pillow held over her face, just possibly in her sleep.

"When Blake was on the stand, he was not his own best witness. And the smart boy, the young Assistant D.A. made him look like a lecherous dog. He led him, and I mean led, to the point of admitting he'd finished up all his other calls, waiting till the last to enjoy his call on Ellie. Funny thing—the fact that Ellie needed saving was held more against him than in his favor.

"That was roughly where we had got by adjournment the day before Theodore Adkins showed up in my office with a lush named Michael Regan, the surprise witness. I was very, very glad to meet them both.

"All along, Blake had maintained a witness existed who could corroborate his story of having been home by ten-thirty. But he would not name him. Just how Adkins went about rounding up Regan, I don't know. I didn't want to know. But Michael Regan sober, as he admittedly had not been often in recent times, testified to having gone to see the Reverend Blake that fatal night, to having sat upon his brownstone stoop until the Reverend showed up at half-past ten, and to having spent the next hour with him confessing to all sorts of sins, including beating his wife. Conveniently, Regan had again fallen from grace. We were able to offer his wife in corroborating testimony. She had a fresh batch of bruises which the judge viewed in his chamber. Whereupon he decided it unnecessary to proceed. Tidy, isn't it? We can prove Regan beats his wife as he said he does. Therefore he's an honest man."

"Tidier than justice sometimes is," Jimmie said.

"Justice is as relative as sin and you know it, my boy," Mumford said.

Jimmie nodded in reluctant agreement. "What denomination is the Reverend Blake?"

"Mongrel, I'd say, a mongrelarian."

Jimmie grinned. "You're an irreligious bastard."

"No, I'm conservative in politics, orthodox in religion, and I have five children by the same woman."

"Didn't anyone question an Irishman's confession to a Protestant clergyman?"

"To an evangelist," Mumford corrected. "There's a distinction. Only an evangelist gets through to a drunkard. They both live in worlds of exaggerated reality. I am sure Michael Regan blackened his wife's eye to prove he was a gentleman—in not smashing her mouth. No one doubted his story, any more than they would question his confessor. Why City Hall is a virtual hotbed of orthodoxy, man, but an evangelist can get Times Square for his pulpit. Yes, and I've no doubt the loan of the Vice Squad to pass the collection plates along Broadway."

Jimmie laughed and signaled the waiter for the check.

15

When Tully mentioned to the D.A.'s secretary that he was going to see Mrs. Mellody who had a club for matrimonial availables, he got a nod and then a sudden response. Mary Ryan had been in the District Attorney's office since she finished business college.

"Jasp, wait a minute. Mellody Friendship Club—is that it?"

"That's it." He went back to her desk and stood rubbing the back of his neck. There was such a nagging familiarity to the name. "Do we have something on them?"

"The murder of Ellie True," Miss Ryan said.

"My gosh, I knew that!" Tully cried, and allowed a slow great smile to crawl all over his face. It made his ugly visage a joy to see.

Miss Ryan hated to spoil matters. "Wait till you get into it," she said. "It's not all that pretty." She began getting out the files for him.

Tully took them into his office, and when one of the men who had worked on the case came in, Miss Ryan sent him in to Tully. By then the latter had lost much of his enthusiasm, just as she had prophesied. Every member of the Mellody Club at the time, including Mrs. Sperling and George Allan Masters, had been checked out. Genuine, strong alibis.

The investigator told Tully what he already knew: the last person they wanted to charge with murder was a clergyman. But the heat was on over the rackets, and Ellie True was a good name with which to attract the public attention. Also, one hell of a good case had been collected against Alfonzo Blake.

"And you know something, Jasp? I still think we had the right man. That's why the thing's been quiet ever since. But what happened, just as Junior was about to nail things down for the prosecution. . .('Junior' was the uncomplimentary nickname the old timers in the office gave to one of the assistant D.A.'s). . .just at the critical minute, some damn fool millionaire philanthropist had to get in on the act.

"No connection with the case whatever. Never heard of the Mellody Club in his life. Read in the papers that poor old Reverend Blake couldn't compromise his holy office by naming a witness. So out he went and scoured the streets until he found the witness or a reasonable facsimile thereof. He pushed that poor slob Regan into court to swear he was confessing wife-beating to Blake down on Fourth Street at the very hour we said Blake was holding a pillow over Ellie's face.

"Well, Jasp, Junior couldn't say soap for blowing bubbles, and to make things tougher he was up against Elmo Mumford, and you know what a killer that guy is when he smells blood." He shook his hands, palms down, at the files. "It's all in there, God help us."

"Any idea where Blake is now?" Tully asked.

The other investigator shrugged. "We can put a line on him if you like."

"We better do that, and just for the hell of it, I'll see if we can pick up Regan."

"That's a long time ago for a man with his thirst, Jasp."

"Maybe I can buy him a drink."

"What about the millionaire—Adkins, I think his name was?"

Jasper Tully massaged his chin. "He shouldn't be hard to find if we have to." He grinned. "I'd hate to have him pull the same sort of thing on me he did on you fellows."

Tully began his exploration of the files. He did not relish the prospect of tracking down all these people, members of the Mellody Club at the time. He wondered if any of them still belonged to it. He doubted it. One name had been crossed from the list before the alibi check had even begun: Edward T. Murdock, Grover Hotel, had left New York for Sando, Ohio, two days before the murder.

16

Tully ate a good meal too fast, but he got to the Friendship Club just as most of its members were arriving for the evening. He suspected he looked right at home himself. All he needed do was give his hat a twist in his hand while he waited. He tried it. Sure enough, that got him a winsome smile from a great innocent lump of a woman. Tully sighed. The world was loaded with innocents, and none the better for it.

 He watched Mrs. Mellody amble her amiable way toward him. She treated all her visitors like children whether they were twice or half her age. Suddenly he realized she had been sizing him up from the moment she came out the kitchen door. Her clients might think he belonged, but she had him pegged for a cop before she was across the room.

"I wonder if you don't have a good notion why I'm here, Mrs. Mellody?"

"I'm sure it's something we had better speak of in private," she said. "I don't like my people disturbed."

"I wasn't thinking of disturbing them, ma'am. I don't suppose it takes much to make them want to fly away, does it?"

She had been about to take him upstairs. She changed her mind. "Maybe we can sit in what we call The Little Parlor. I see applicants for membership in there. When they can hear the laughter and the music and the clatter of plates, it encourages them to want to join us. We are a family in many ways—the only family some of us will ever know." She scarcely changed her tone of voice. "It is the Sperling woman you want to speak of, officer?"

"That's it, all right."

"She was one of those who left us after the Ellie True affair."

"Well, I'm glad of that for your sake, Mrs. Mellody. It'll save you some questioning anyway."

She looked at him. An open-faced woman, she might be shrewd, but she was also frank, and appreciated the quality in others. "I do believe you are," she said. "What is your name again, officer?"

"Jasper Tully."

Her mind was always far in advance of her speech. "One of the people I misjudged in my time—and I don't often misjudge so far as the interests of the house are concerned—was Arabella Sperling. She was a human spider. She would intrigue a man into her web and sit back watching him perform for her. She would poke and prod. Oh, very unpleasant. I should have asked her to leave many a time, but it wasn't that simple. I think she might have tried to pull the house down about us. Smiling, of course, while she did it. I must say I'm not surprised at what happened to her. I could have strangled her myself many a time."

"Do you know anyone else who felt that way about her, Mrs. Mellody?"

"No. I lost complete track of her. I don't suppose I heard of her since—until her death."

"But I mean at the time she was here, did anyone, to your knowledge, come to really hate her?"

Mrs. Mellody thought more carefully of that. "I suppose all our boys—all the men, that is—must have been glad to escape her attentions."

"Anyone particular?" Tully persisted.

"No...o," she said still with a note of qualification.

"Anyone still with you who was in the club in her day?"

"Not a soul, I'm happy to say. By which I mean, Mr. Tully, we like to see people depart from us able to stand up to, and participate in, an aggressive society."

Onward Christian Soldiers, Tully thought. He brought from his coat pocket the list of mourners who had put in an appearance at the funeral parlor. "Any names here you recognize, Mrs. Mellody?"

The big woman fetched a pair of nose glasses on a string from somewhere in the depth of her bosom and studied the list. A show of recognition came to her face. "George Allan Masters. He was one of ours. Oh, dear. . .a nice man. Divorced from a horrid wife at the time. I went into that. I have to, you see. So many of our people don't approve of divorce. And if there are children, it makes such complications. But then of course, we don't get many divorces. The economic station of most of our people doesn't encourage it. But George was one of those she wanted particularly to coax into her parlor."

"When did he leave the Friendship Club?"

"Under the happiest of circumstances. He married one of our new girls, a woman a bit older than himself."

One of the new old girls, Tully thought. Since Masters was solidly alibied for the night of Mrs. Sperling's murder, there was no point in searching him. "Now, what about Dr. Alfonzo Blake?"

"That man," Mrs. Mellody said with consummate scorn.

"Didn't he fit in?"

"He did not, though he belonged to us. He joined strictly for purposes of his own, I do believe, and I don't think they had anything to do with the Lord's work. Oh, I don't suppose that's fair to him either. He needed all the sources of income he could find to scratch out a living. And not much of a living it was. I never knew a man so thin. If he'd swallowed a needle, you'd see the bulge."

Tully smiled.

"You have a nice face when you smile, Mr. Tully."

"Kind of awful without it though, isn't it?" he drawled. "Was there any particular friendship between Blake and Mrs. Sperling?"

"No, none. The only half-way special friend Blake had was Eddie Murdock. And what they had in common was a matter of considerable worry to me——." Mrs. Mellody leaned forward and put a finger on his arm that Tully thought would pin down any man. "They both liked 'girls'. . .young girls."

Her eyes were glistening, and it wasn't nice to see. She was the worst kind of puritan. Nothing must give her more pleasure than to arrange a sexless marriage.

"Well," Tully said, getting up, "I guess it was better for them than liking boys, at that."

17

Jimmie had not finished dressing in the morning when Mrs. Norris tapped on his bedroom door. He wondered if she was on a tea "kick" again. Periodically she took to urging a cup of morning tea upon him while he was dressing. He absolutely refused to pour it over himself in bed. The only cure for these morning tea turns of hers was the suggestion that she take a year's leave and go visit Scotland. Likely a good thing for both of them: during her absence he might get married...

"Come in," Jimmie growled.

"Good morning, Mr. James. Your Mr. Adkins is in the study."

"He's where? Did he spend the night there?" It was not yet eight-thirty.

"Certainly not," Mrs. Norris said, with an air of indignity sufficient to his having accused her of spending the night there also.

"All right," Jimmie said, "I'm not blaming you for letting him in."

"But I did," she said, "just a moment ago. He only wants a word with you, a civil word, sir."

"Look, Mrs. Norris, you keep my house. You may even keep my purse, but I will keep my own counsel. Do you understand? Now go out there and get that Teddy-bear out of my study, out of the house. I will see him at the office. Or tell him to come back tonight. No! It's bad enough he's started the day for me. I won't have him ending it, too. Bring me a cup of coffee."

"Yes, sir. I'll take him one, too."

"I want mine first!" Jimmie cried.

Mrs. Norris turned round. "I have ever done everything for you first, Master Jamie," she said reproachfully.

Jimmie sat down and held his head in his hands until the coffee arrived. It was one hell of a way to start the day.

Adkins was delicately sipping his coffee out of a blue china cup, and with a silver coffee service gleaming beside him. It was enough to blind a man at that hour. He was pouring himself a second cup when Jimmie joined him. He offered one to his host.

Jimmie accepted limply.

"I should like to have my clipping book back if you're through with it—and Mama has sent you an invitation."

"Thanks," Jimmie said, brightening a bit. After all, it might have been Mama herself who turned up in his study.

"She thought you might like to spend the week-end with us. She said I should recommend our hunting."

"Do you hunt?"

"Oh, no," Adkins said. "I don't approve killing for pleasure."

Jimmie unlocked the middle drawer of his desk and brought out the album. He returned it to its owner.

"Find anything interesting?"

"What put you onto the Ellie True affair?"

"I liked the looks of the unfortunate Reverend Blake. He resembled Don Quixote. And Ellie True reminded me of my sister, Miranda."

"You knew them then?"

"Certainly not, except as they appeared in the newspapers. I am an avid reader and clipper." He glanced at his watch. "I must get along to the office. Will you call Mama today about the week-end? She would like you to come up on Friday." He tucked the album into his dispatch case.

"I'll call," Jimmie said.

"I don't suppose you're going downtown now?"

"Not yet," Jimmie said. He simply could not bring himself to invite the man to wait or to share his breakfast with him. He took him to the door. The most hospitable thing he could manage was a weak smile.

He picked up the morning paper and took it to the table with him.

Mrs. Norris served him an egg, the collar of which had

a brown fringe on it. "The pan was too hot," she explained unnecessarily. "You could have asked Mr. Adkins to breakfast. I always have enough eggs in the house."

"There's been enough of Mr. Adkins in the house, too," Jimmie said.

"I think he's a very cheerful gentleman, and it's nice to see one here, especially in the morning."

"He reminds me of Harpo Marx," Jimmie said, "scalped."

"I think that's disgusting, sir."

"So do I!" roared Jimmie, and watched her thump out of the room.

18

Mrs. Norris sat a few moments before doing the dishes that morning although it was a practice she disapproved in others, much less herself. But Mr. Adkins, arriving that early had nonetheless remembered the book he had promised her: Ballads of the North Countrie. She read a few lines here and there. . ."And the birk and the broom blooms bonnie. . ." Where else in the world over was there such a resounding use of the language?

She rose to the ring of the telephone. It was Mr. Adkins himself. "I'm about to impose on you for a most enormous favor," he said. "I wonder if you could take an hour from your day, and help me select a gift for my mother? She's a very old lady, and I thought perhaps something in Scotch wool. . ."

Mrs. Norris could not very well refuse him. So they met at eleven at Lord & Taylor. Before reaching the woolens, Mr. Adkins caused them to peruse a few things in silk and some jewelry in gold and silver. He had lovely taste for a man, and almost fondled the things he fancied, she observed, and she remembered that he had the pocketbook to match his taste, according to Mr. James.

"Are you sure it's a very old lady, sir?" Mrs. Norris ventured once indirectly commenting on a trinket with which he was trifling.

Mr. Adkins laughed. "I swear it by my honor and hers." While they awaited the elevator, he asked: "Has Mr. Jarvis told you of the scrape I'm in?"

"No, sir. Mr. James never confides his clients' affairs to me.

"'Tis a woman, you know," Adkins said, and Mrs. Norris was aware of his sidelong glance to see how she took it.

"Many a man gets scraped by them, if he takes up with too sharp a one," she said. She was pleased with herself for having been right in her guess about him the first night he came into the house.

"Oh that I'd had the benefit of such wisdom in time," Adkins cried. "I did but call on her a few times—properly, I assure you—and now she dares accuse me of fathering her child."

An elevator was no place to pursue that subject, and in truth, Mrs. Norris was glad of the respite to cover the pause it gave her. "The old ballads are lovely," she said on the way up. "All about courting and dueling, parting and pledging. I never knew the Scotch were so great on poisons."

Mr. Adkins, close by her side in the elevator, gave her arm a little squeeze while he laughed. "You are a delightful woman."

They ended up buying Mama a Sea Isle sweater, and Mr. Adkins said it was a shame to have brought Mrs. Norris out of the house to select something he could have bought through the Sunday magazine section of *The New York Times*. The least he could do now if she would allow it, was take her to lunch.

"I know a place where the salmon melts on your tongue," he coaxed.

Mrs. Norris, allowing that she would have to eat somewhere, consented. She even found herself wishing that by some marvel of fate, Jasper Tully might chance to see them. But then it would get to Mr. James, and she would as soon that not happen. And the fact that she felt that way troubled her. Not enough to ruin her appetite, but enough to disturb her digestion.

Which was altogether nonsense. Mr. Adkins was merely paying a debt he had not needed to contract, and doing it graciously.

"Am I not in a shocking predicament?" he said after a pause between fish and dessert.

She supposed his mind went back to his trouble at every idle moment. And then she suddenly realized why he was so much about the house and her: he needed the protection he felt came from being near Mr. James, poor man. She could entirely understand that. It was a terrible thing to be accused of, and you innocent.

"I don't rightly know how far it can go," she said, referring to the paternity suit. "Isn't there some medical proof?"

"I do believe that from the type of blood they could prove my innocence if the child's type and mine are different. But if they're the same, it's all up to the jury—and Mr. Jarvis."

"Should you be admitting that even if it's so?" Mrs. Norris asked, having been trained to a healthy reverence for the forms of law.

"Only in the bosom of my friends."

He was not in her bosom by some distance, Mrs. Norris thought, not caring much for such intimacy of speech. "There's many a viper in the bosom of friends," she advised.

"I should rather die than consent to such cynicism!" Adkins cried melodramatically. "Where can we turn if not to our friends? Shall I turn back to the wretch who deliberately cast me into this situation? I will not. She would marry me tomorrow, young vixen that she is. But I will not have her!"

His face was flushed with the vehemence of his protest. Mrs. Norris made what she hoped were soothing noises, and advised him, somewhat uselessly at this stage: "You should leave the young ones alone, Mr. Adkins. With a man of your maturity and your station, they are up to no good."

"I am not one who cares one fig about station," Mr. Adkins scored while he had the chance. "A man can be as well clipped in a castle as in a cottage."

"Oh, better," Mrs. Norris said. "It's the cottages which get even the castling kind in trouble."

"My sister married a count," Adkins said. "She's home now with Mama."

"And I dare say, with a packet of children?"

"And grandchildren!" Adkins said.

Mrs. Norris thought about that for a moment. "She didn't come right home then, did she?"

"I suppose I do exaggerate for the sake of a story," he admitted.

"There," Mrs. Norris said, spooning up the last bit of sherbet, "I must get home myself to the work I'm paid for doing."

"And I down to the work for which I am over-paid," Adkins said. "Do you know, I have never altogether approved the broker's profession? One makes money in it out of other people's money."

"'Tis better than making it out of blood," Mrs. Norris said.

Mr. Adkins' round blue eyes narrowed upon her. "My dear Mrs. Norris, just what does that mean?"

"I'm referring to the munitions makers, millions out of guns the world over."

"How admirable you are," he said, with a new flush of color bursting into his cheeks. "And I suppose you are right: it is better to make money out of money. Money does labor hard, you know, in our times. If you have any, I trust it's working for you. It will get on with the chore when you're worn out."

"I never quite thought of it that way," she said.

"In that manner of speaking," Adkins said, "a broker is worth his fee. But there, I sound like a drummer, don't I?"

"Are brokers interested in the widow's mite?" Mrs. Norris asked tentatively while she put on her gloves.

"Mites are mighty," he said, "if you know what I mean."

"I do. I've heard it said that women like myself, if they all voted together, could control some of the biggest corporations in the nation."

Adkins merely nodded, as though himself mute in wonder at it. Finally, paying the check, and leaving a tip the size of which Mrs. Norris approved if the waiter did not, he laid his hand a moment on her gloved one. "If ever you need advice," he said, "I should be glad to offer it. The widow's friend, you might say. And I'd waive my usual fee in your case." He fluttered his hands like a butterfly and dismissed the matter. "That is all! Let us speak no more of money, but rather of old ballads. . ." He almost sang the line to her: "'Get up and bar the door.'"

He had beautiful hands, she thought, long and delicate, unlike the rest of him. They were the kind to be seen on Christmas cards, the thumbs pointing up to heaven.

"Ha!" she said, "'Get up and bar the door!' I'd better at that!"

19

It was peculiar summary of herself Mrs. Norris got when she took inventory that afternoon. For the life of her she could not imagine why she should so enjoy the company of Mr. Adkins. She could not really say she liked the man, and she had never been one to coax flattery of herself. By their stations, she had no business socializing with the man at all. The plain fact was she had enjoyed herself thinking it might tweak the nose of someone who couldn't see beyond it when he had it into a case. Three days without a word from Jasper Tully. He probably thought she would meddle if he came round. The old grouch must think she loved him for himself alone! And that was a thought to make anyone shocked with herself.

"Annie Norris, shame," she bade herself. The truth was she was jealous of a dead woman, and one murdered in her bed at that.

When Jimmie brought his drink in to the kitchen table while she was getting dinner, and said: "Mrs. Norris, how would you like to do a bit of detective work for me?" her world suddenly righted itself.

"I wouldn't mind if I'm able," she said.

"I shall have to take you into my confidence about our Theodore Adkins," Jimmie started.

For a moment Mrs. Norris wondered if she should stop him. There seemed to be something not quite straight about it. She had that very day told Mr. Adkins that Mr. Jarvis did not confide such affairs to her. But Jimmie was already into it, and there seemed to be nothing new in the content so she listened him out as he told the substance of the suit.

"I've now reached the point," he concluded, "where I feel I've got to know something about the woman, Daisy Thayer. She works at Mark Stewart's on Fifth Avenue at the perfume counter. In fact, that's where Adkins met her..."

He was not a man who could pass up a perfume counter without a sniff of appreciation; Mrs. Norris knew that from experience.

"...I don't know just how you'll go about this," Jimmie went on. "You might ask Jasper for some advice." Jimmie knew from the ruffle of her shoulders that she would not. Tully and she must be on the outs.

"There's nothing to being a good detective but knowing when to ask questions and when to keep your mouth shut," she said.

"You're hired," said Jimmie, which Mrs. Norris knew was only a manner of speaking. But she was to have extra an expense account.

20

After working his way through most of the parishes in the Village and Chelsea, Jasper Tully finally got a line on Michael Regan, the surprise witness in the Ellie True case. He had thought from the first that an Irishman's telling his sins to a Protestant evangelist was both unholy and unlikely. It was not much of a line he got, to be sure, Regan having, soon after his testimony had saved the Reverend Blake, himself gone to the grave, and that of a drunkard. He had fallen up a four inch curbstone and split open his head. All that he left behind was a mourning widow.

She was still grieving when Tully went to see her. He knew the type all the way from his childhood: the only time they'd make up to a man was when he lay flat with lumbago or stretched in his coffin. The late Michael Regan would have had his sympathy.

"Ach, don't be raking poor Mike's bones over, Mr. Tully," she keened. "He did beat me, 'tis true, but it was his way of loving when the beast was up in him, and I'd never've made it a matter of public notice if it wasn't for the bit of money in it."

"You were paid then for giving testimony in the Blake case?"

"Only an allowance to make us fit for public appearance, a few dollars, Mr. Tully. Nothing to be disturbing poor Michael now over."

"Did your benefactor come to you himself?"

"Oh, no. He went to Michael, Mr. Adkins did, or his representative."

"Did you ever see the Reverend Blake?"

"I'm not sure, except in court that day. But I might have, living down the street from him then."

"Do you know where he lives now?"

"Why should I, and him a Protestant?"

"You know, Mrs. Regan," Tully drawled, "that's the very thought that's been running through my mind. Now, you can tell me the truth and I don't think it will upset poor Michael wherever he is, or yourself." He leaned forward. She was a woman who loved confidences. "Do you honestly believe Michael confessed his sins to a Protestant clergyman?"

"Oh, I do that, Mr. Tully. When Michael 'ud get a crying jag on, he'd confess his sins to the President of the United States on the White House steps."

Tully swore to himself and returned to his office in as glum a mood as had obsessed him in many a day. He settled into melancholy contemplation of the case. So often it was the little things, the little fragments of physical evidence. For example there was the piece of jewelry still missing, something called a "lover's knot": According to the nieces it was missing, and he was willing to take their word on an inventory of their inheritance. He scarcely lifted his chin from his breast when the detective who had worked on the Ellie True case stuck his head in the door.

"Whisst, Jasper."

Tully glowered at him from under ominous brows. "What do you want?"

"Would you like to talk to the Reverend Alfonzo Blake?"

"Yes, I would."

"Now?"

Tully unfolded his knotted shape like a ripened nut. "Where did you find him?"

"Well, I'm half-ashamed and half-proud of myself. I searched records and galleries, and put out lines to this bureau and that, and then sat down on my backside like you to think. And while I was sitting, I noticed the telephone book. And that's where I found him."

Alfonzo Blake was a man as long and lean as himself, Tully noted, and he came into the room a bit stooped and wary, with the attitude of having bumped his head on too many doorways. His cheeks were sunken, his black eyes bright as a fanatic's. He had not had an easy time of it his fifty odd years on earth. The detective motioned him into the chair opposite him, across the desk.

"I appreciate your coming in," Tully started.

"I should have appreciated not coming in here again ever," Blake said in a voice the vibration of which was strong enough to tremble the pictures on the wall. "I have never offended society, but its representatives have grievously offended me."

"You should have been District Attorney with that voice," Tully said, trying to lighten the weight of their visit.

"Have I been summoned here for vocational guidance? It's too late for that."

"How long is it since you saw Arabella Sperling?"

Blake repeated the name and closed his eyes in thought. When he opened them it was obvious he had remembered her, and with sudden and great expectation. "She's dead?"

"She's dead," Tully said.

The man strove for piety of mien, but he moistened his lips as though he could taste...what? Money, of course.

"She was murdered," Tully added, and in that instant watched something die in the man opposite him. He had expected an inheritance! The poor devil was turning green: he was now expecting much worse than nothing.

"Oh, no," Blake murmured folding his arms across his thin chest in self-fortification.

"Now you understand why I want to talk to you."

The Reverend Blake nodded.

"You knew she had money," Tully said.

"At the Mellody Club she made no secret of it," Blake said.

"That was advertising for trouble, wasn't it?" Tully said.

"She was advertising for a husband."

"And wasn't there anyone willing to take her up on it?"

"I suppose most every man in the place thought about it now and then."

"Did you?"

"No, sir."

"Are you unmarried, Reverend?"

"I am a celibate."

Tully nodded, admitting the distinction. "Was Mrs. Mellody called as a character witness for you in the Ellie True business?"

"She was, and precious little character she left me," he said bitterly. "If ever a witness was led by an attorney she was by your office. 'Oh, a very honest man,' said she, 'in matters of money, that is. And a very sincere one about his religion.' 'Then you would trust him?' said the District Attorney. 'With my purse,' said she. 'Would you trust him with your daughter, Madam?' Objection. Objection sustained. But Madam tumbled out a few voluntary words which the judge could strike till doomsday without having stricken: 'I do not have a daughter, for which in this instant I thank God.'"

"You must have been very glad to see Michael Regan turn up in court," Tully said matter-of-factly.

"I prayed him into court."

"It's too bad you couldn't have saved his life when you got out of court," Tully drawled.

"Believe me, I would have tried if I could have found him."

"Would you have recognized him if you saw him?"

Blake's eyes met the investigator's and held. "Yes, sir."

"Why didn't you try this millionaire fellow, this Adkins? He'd found him the first time."

"I never saw Adkins—before, during, or after my trial. He wrote me a congratulatory letter after it was over. He wished me a long and provident ministry."

"Did he endow it?"

For the first time, Blake smiled. "Only with his blessing. I had thought at the time that if I were a criminal, he might have contributed something toward my rehabilitation. It was an ungrateful thought. But though my life is founded and grounded on the Good Book, I have always felt a certain sympathy for the prodigal's brother."

A humanity that, in the man of the cloth, which Tully liked. He got a good feeling about him in spite of himself, and he could understand the philanthropist's being moved by him to the point of trying to prove his alibi for him. On the whole, he was glad not to have been himself on the case: he would not like to have had a part in bringing Alfonzo Blake to trial, and he was sufficiently humble to know that he might not then have had the perceptivity about the clergyman he now had.

"I'm not much of a Bible man," Tully said, "but I know what you mean." He got up and straightened a picture that seemed to have been tilted by the other man's big voice. "It's a terrible thing to have to stand up in that dock and face the charge of murder. Especially when you can't name someone who might prove your innocence."

"Your office has a graver responsibility in such cases," Blake said, trying to pull himself out of the limelight.

"We try hard not to make mistakes like that one," Tully said, looking down at him. "But maybe somebody helped us—without you knowing it or us knowing it. If you didn't kill the woman, somebody did, and that somebody liked it just fine, you being tried for it. The trouble with such mistakes, Mr. Blake, sometimes they never get righted. The murder of Ellie True hasn't been solved yet.

"Now nobody must have thought about that more than you, sir. You're an honest man of God. I want an answer straight from you—who do you think murdered Ellie True?"

"No one of my acquaintance, sir."

"That's not a straight answer."

"I don't know! That's straight enough for law. It should be for you."

"Then let me put a bug in your ear, Reverend, and see if it tickles your memory. You weren't the only lecher in Mrs. Mellody's books. She didn't like that pal of yours, Eddie Murdock, who somehow managed to have left town that night. There doesn't come any alibi better than that. I want to know something from you, Mr. Blake—didn't you wonder, too, if Eddie Murdock was really out of town?"

"Maybe I did in my desperation, God help me, but I was ashamed of myself for it."

"Why?"

"Because of my own guilt! Of course, I ogled girls! I lusted after women, and I flayed myself for it, I persecuted my flesh like a medieval monk. And I often felt Murdock's company was thrust upon me by the Lord God Almighty to try my soul. . ." Too much saliva had gathered in the man's mouth and made an ugly rasping sound when he drew in his breath. The veins were standing out on his forehead. "And Murdock would sit, his lips soft and wet as liver, and he would say under his breath—oh, terrible sensual things about one and another of the women, and especially Ellie True."

"All right," Tully said, "Take it easy."

He went himself to the files. Lips like liver. The picture of it turned his own stomach. He had a rare gift of speech, the Reverend Blake.

Tully searched the records for any mention at all of Murdock. There was none except the notation authorizing the deletion of his name from the list of suspects. He had checked out of the Grover Hotel, having purchased his railway ticket for Sando, Ohio, through the hotel. According to a wire check with the sheriff there, Murdock was in Sando on the date Ellie True was murdered.

What could you do with that, Tully wondered: as neat as a bald head. "Did the police question you about Murdock at all?"

"They did not."

"And of course, you wouldn't have volunteered your suspicions to them."

"Mr. Tully, you must understand: I had no suspicions of him or anyone else at that time. It was only after I was arrested, and while I was casting about desperately trying to discover what had happened to me, how I had come to be in such a predicament."

"And it occurred to you then that you might have been framed?"

Blake sat forward in the chair, his long legs collapsed like a dog on its haunches. "As God is my witness, that never occurred to me until this very minute."

"Think about it," Tully said.

"Oh, I am." Blake rolled his head about in an agony of recollection. The evangelist's exhibitionism, Tully thought, watching him. "It was he who told me where she lived…and when she would be there, likely alone."

"And you couldn't think of that to tell to the police when you were on trial for your life?"

Blake shook his head. "Unless you knew Murdock, you wouldn't know how subtle he had been with that insinuation. And don't you see I was blinded by guilt. If Ellie True would have had me that night, I would have sinned!"

Tully was on the verge of saying he wouldn't have been the first man, but there was not much point to that. "Did you ever see or hear of Murdock since?"

"Never."

"What was his business, do you know?"

"I should have supposed a salesman of some sort. I met him at the Friendship Club. He was better spoken than most men I've known. And I do remember he had certain little exercises he could do with his hands—'magician language,' he called it once. He might very well have been an entertainer, come to think of it. And he was certainly wise to the ways of the world."

"Let's have a description of him," Tully said, remembering the already described lips.

"About fifty, a little plump, but the kind of man one would expect to be a good dancer. He looked to have taken the best of care of himself. Sandy hair, which, to tell the truth, I often wondered about: it might possibly have been a transformation..."

Tully grinned as he wrote the word. He hadn't heard it since the dear dead days almost beyond recall when he read *Andy Gump*.

"...And the most unusual thing about him, I suppose, was his walk, as though all his weight went on his heels. A walk is hard to disguise, isn't it?"

"It sure is," Tully said, his old heart pumping. "Some men have walked to the electric chair."

Tully could not get the Reverend Blake out of his office fast enough after that. As soon as he was gone, the investigator checked with the Grover Hotel. It was small, but clean, and not at all the sort of place to arrange transportation for its residents. It was, in fact, a residential hotel with a long waiting list, and Edward T. Murdock had been expected to live there for at least some months when he got in. Instead he stayed but two weeks although he paid a month's rent. No one remembered having arranged his transportation, but if it had been an emergency, say a death in the family, likely the desk clerk would have done it as a courtesy.

Most of this came from the manager's deduction. No one remembered him. The records showed only the dates of his occupancy.

Tully called Mrs. Mellody. "How long did that fellow Murdock belong to your club?"

"Off-hand I should say six or seven months."

"That long," Tully murmured. "Did he give you reference?"

"I should certainly think so," she said. "Do you want me to look it up?"

"Do, please, ma'am," Tully said, "and call me back at this number." While he waited, he checked the Guild of Variety Artists for Edward T. Murdock. No record. He called the Society of Magicians. The Society did have a member by that name. He was known as Murdock the Mighty, and his home address was Box 17, Sando, Ohio.

"Where the hell is Sando, Ohio?" Tully cried out as soon as he got off the phone.

By then the office secretary, Miss Ryan, had come in to help him, making notes as he gave them. She volunteered to call the Automobile Club. Sando was twenty miles southeast of Columbus.

"So that's where he landed," Tully said, in sudden good humor.

"Where who landed?" Miss Ryan murmured.

"Americus Vespucci."

"Who?"

"'Who's on first,'" Tully said.

Miss Ryan shook her head and took her notes to the typewriter. Tully's humor wasn't the variety of Irish to which she had been raised.

The switchboard girl came to the door. "A Mrs. Mellody is on number three, Mr. Tully."

"Thank you, darling," said Tully and took the phone.

"Eddie Murdock gave as reference the president of the Society of Magicians," she said. "I certainly should have remembered that. The reason I accepted him in the first place was my hope that he might entertain us a bit."

Free, Tully thought. "And did he?"

"No. Not ever."

"What address did he give you when he applied for admission?"

"Membership, not admission, Mr. Tully. Why, the address on his application is the Grover Hotel."

"And the date?"

Mrs. Mellody gave it. Eddie Murdock had used that address six months before he moved into the hotel, probably from the day he got on their waiting list. Curious and confusing. Tully thanked the woman and hung up.

He swung around on his swivel chair. "Miss Ryan, where's the Big Man? I want his authorization for a flying trip to—where am I going? Sando, Ohio."

He took his supper at the airport, and finding himself with almost a half hour before flight time, he walked about and thought of some of the things he should have done and hadn't. His eyes fell on the push-button flight insurance machine. He put in his coin and took out twenty-five thousand dollars' worth. Making out the application, he put down Mrs. Annie Norris as beneficiary. He then went to a phone booth and called her.

It was Jimmie who answered.

"I suppose I should hang up," Tully said. "You know, 'if a man answers. . .' Could I speak to Mrs. Norris, Jimmie? I'm calling from the airport."

"I'm sorry, Jasp. She's not here. Any message?"

Tully grunted his disappointment. "Tell her I just put her down as beneficiary on my life insurance."

"That should cheer her up," Jimmie said.

"Downcast these days, is she?" Tully said, feeling good about that at least.

"You don't come around as often as you used to," said Jimmie.

"There's answer to that one, too," Tully said, "but you never can tell these days where your telephone conversation is going to turn up. Okay, my lad. I'm off to see a magician about a man. I'll be back in a day or two."

"I'll give her your love."

"Do, and a smack where she'll forget-me-not."

21

Mrs. Norris started her assignment for Jimmie by a scouting expedition. She joined the morning crowd of shoppers pushing into Mark Stewart's. She was shocked by their number. In the old days Mark Stewart's had the air of a cathedral. It was no better now than an air terminus...which reminded her that she would like to have been home the night before to hear what Mr. Tully had to say for himself.

She saw the perfume counter and studied the girls behind it. Between the hair-dos and the face-dos, they had managed to trim themselves to the looks of youth. But they'd have to be careful, especially of their smiles cracking open the makeup. And a cautious smile was no smile at all. Like a kiss at a charity ball. Which one was Daisy Thayer, she wondered.

Daisy. The only creature she had ever known by the name was a spotted cow. And, she thought now, she'd as soon have her acquaintance. She turned to the umbrella counter. There was but one clerk on duty there, and she was a cloudy day.

The counter opposite was gloves. That was the place for her, Mrs. Norris decided. The little stools gave it an air of permanency. Mrs. Norris took up her position on one of them.

"I want someone to wait on me who has been with Stewart's a while," she said, in her best Victorian manner. "I am an old customer, and I know what I want."

"I'll get Mrs. Shaw for you," the young woman said. "She's been here for ages."

Mrs. Norris gave her a neat smile, and settled herself more firmly on the stool. She began to remove long buttoned kid gloves which she had had to get out of the trunk that morning. She had determined to go out of the house a lady, no matter how the day might send her back into it.

Mrs. Shaw came up, managing a chill smile. Nothing bode so ill of a customer to a seasoned clerk than her assurance that she knew what she wanted.

Mrs. Norris said: "How d'you do," and described the gloves she was looking for.

They were easily found and fitted, much to the clerk's pleasure, and easily paid for, to Mrs. Norris', since Mr. James would do it. Having attended that pair, and finding out on the way that Mrs. Shaw was a widow who had reared three children while working in Stewart's, Mrs. Norris asked for something to wear in the evening. "My son takes me out now and then," she said, and put a brave face on what she hoped was not the biggest lie she had ever told.

"What does he do?" Mrs. Shaw asked and volunteered in the same breath: "I have a boy living home, too. He's an actor."

Mrs. Norris threw her hands in the air. "Now isn't that remarkable! My Jamie's an actor, too."

"What's his name?" Mrs. Shaw said. "Should I know him?"

"Well, you should," Mrs. Norris said hesitantly, an attitude, it turned out, easily understood by the mother of an actor.

"I know," Mrs. Shaw said soothingly. "He's at liberty, isn't he? Arnold has been very lucky. Arnold Shaw's his name."

"I've heard of him," Mrs. Norris said, and she had just then if not before. "Is he playing in something now?"

"As a matter of fact, he's opening in a play tonight, *Raggle Toggle Tom*. You may have seen about it in the papers. It's off-Broadway, and I say, that's better than on. You know where you are for more than the one night. It's a nice play and he has a lovely part in it. He's a very good actor."

"I'm sure he is," Mrs. Norris said. "You can have all the radio and all the television and all the moving pictures. Give me a good play with real, live actors."

"Ah, Madam, it does my heart good to talk to a woman like you. Hold up your hand, dear."

Mrs. Shaw leaned close, pulling down the glove she was fitting, and Mrs. Norris said into her ear: "The dark-haired girl at the perfume counter—haven't I seen her somewhere?"

"She says she's a model."

"What's her name?"

Mrs. Shaw mentioned it and Mrs. Norris bit her lip; she had got the wrong one.

"The blonde looks familiar, too."

"Maybe you've seen her in pictures," Mrs. Shaw said, "but if you did, you're the only one I know who has. And we've been watching, I can tell you. Miss Daisy Thayer, that is. She's back on the job here after a year in Hollywood. Or so she says. My Arnold says she may have been—the hidden item on somebody's expense account, if you know what I mean."

"It would be hard to hide something like that," Mrs. Norris said. A year, she thought: time enough to package a baby, poor thing. "And Stewart's hired her back?"

"Oh the men swarm round her like bees, and it's them buy the perfume, you know." Mrs. Shaw gave her customer's hand a pinch. "Arnold used to come into the store now and then. He's very handsome if I do say so. That was the first time she noticed that I also was on this planet. She would smile over at me as though she had a lump of sugar between her teeth. Arnold took her out several times, and I never interfered. Then all of a sudden, she couldn't see him for gold dust. A man half Arnold's size and twice his age. With my own eyes I watched her pick him up."

"Did you? She must be a bold thing to have done it right in front of you."

"Not only that. When she came back from having lunch with him that first time, on her relief she went up to a friend in the Credit Department for information on him. And you know what kind of information they have up there."

"What kind?" said Mrs. Norris.

"Well, it's not going to tell her whether he goes to church on Sunday."

"Of course not," said Mrs. Norris. "It would be his financial status."

"It would give his bank and credit references, and his home address which was Weston, Connecticut, and he certainly didn't live there in a bird's nest."

Mrs. Norris wished she had all this in an affidavit. "How do you know she went up to the Credit about him?" she asked, as though she could scarcely conceive a thing so calculating.

"The girl she asked is also a friend of Arnold's so it was right she should tell his mother something like that. And that information is confidential, you know, what Miss Daisy Thayer wanted."

"Couldn't you report her?" Mrs. Norris asked hopefully. The more witnesses the better.

"My dear, it was well over a year ago, all this. Closer to two, you know the way time goes. And at the time, I told it where it would do me and mine the most good. I told it to Arnold. And that put a finish to them."

"Bully for you," Mrs. Norris said with meager enthusiasm. "And did he believe you?"

"He believed her if he doubted me," said the mother. "She wanted no more of him, having Connecticut in tow."

Mrs. Norris wondered how close friends Arnold was now with the girl in the Credit Department, who was also a friend of Daisy's at the time she hooked poor Mr. Adkins.

"I'll take them," Mrs. Norris said of the second pair of gloves. She had never bought two pair at once in her life till now.

"Charge and send?" said Mrs. Shaw.

"Cash and carry," Mrs. Norris said, and counted out a great deal of money. "*Raggle Toggle Tom*—is it a play about gypsies?"

"Oh, no. Tom is a poor little street urchin."

"I don't care much for problem plays," Mrs. Norris said.

"It's not a problem play at all. Not every poor child's a delinquent."

"I would love to see it," Mrs. Norris said. "Maybe I can get my Jamie to take me." Before she left the counter she was persuaded to try to make it that very night when Mrs. Shaw would be there herself, and could introduce them to Arnold.

And before she left the store Mrs. Norris went up to the Credit Department and made out an application for a charge account in the name of somebody she didn't know at an address where no one she did know lived. Meanwhile she studied the girls. She was quite certain she would recognize any of them she saw again. They were all clean and decent and acting themselves only, leaving all the airs to be put on by them opening the charge accounts. There were few things of which Mrs. Norris approved less.

22

"Are you sure that's what she said?" Jimmie insisted. "It's more important than I can tell you."

"I'm in the habit of getting things right," Mrs. Norris said. "Mrs. Shaw said she watched the hussy pick him up herself."

"It isn't her picking him up or putting him down," Jimmie said. "That amounts to hearsay. But that Daisy Thayer went deliberately to check on Theodore Adkins' financial information—that's the thing to hand a jury. What I should like now is an affidavit on it."

"Then take me to the play tonight, Mr. James."

"But I can't do that," Jimmie said. "Don't you understand? Suppose the Thayer woman were to show up herself tonight for this boy's opening—she knows him, doesn't she?—I'm going to be facing her in court, Mrs. Norris."

"Well, Mr. James," she said with Scots doggedness, "if it's below your dignity to do what you ask me to do, all right. It seems to me an excellent opportunity for you to get first hand your ammunition. And tell me this—if she does show up tonight, is that the proper place for the mother of a fatherless child?"

Jimmie had to admit there was something to that. Besides which, Mrs. Norris had touched a sensitive point—his dignity. He was being too bloody zealous of it for his own liking.

"All right," he said. "I'll go."

"Now I'll have to call you by your first name, sir. I've told her you were my son."

"What do I answer to if somebody calls me by my last name?"

Mrs. Norris gave that a moment's thought. "Norris, I suppose."

Jimmie grinned. "Won't you tell me, mother dear, who my father was? I have the right to know."

"Get out of my kitchen!" Mrs. Norris cried, and fanned herself with the evening paper.

Mrs. Shaw was waiting for them near the box office, having every confidence in their arrival. Just before the curtain went up on Raggle Toggle Tom, Mrs. Norris elbowed Jimmie.

"There she is! I was right!"

"Thayer?" said Jimmie.

"No. The girl from the Credit Department of Stewart's, Daisy Thayer's friend, or rather her ex-friend, I'd not be surprised. Here's the way I figured it from something the mother told me: the boy probably went out on a double-date—she's a pretty thing, isn't she?—with her and Daisy. . ."

Jimmie was saved from following Mrs. Norris over the obstacle course of her reasoning by the play's commencement. Sufficient to the needs of the night was the fact that the girl was here, the girl who could testify to Daisy Thayer's calculations. As the play wore on and out, Jimmie thought of several nice things to say to the actors. They, fortunately, were better than their vehicle.

Afterwards, following Mrs. Shaw backstage, Mrs. Norris whispered to Jimmie: "Remember you're an actor, now. Act."

On his introduction to Arnold Shaw, however, Jimmie admitted he was only an occasional actor. He said he was in business.

"That's where all actors should be," Arnold said with a smugness Jimmie found it hard to forgive him. "Mrs. Norris. . .and Mr. Norris, I should like you to meet a friend, Miss Barbara Rossetti."

Miss Rossetti was the girl from the Credit Department. Jimmie took his cue: "What do you say we all have supper together? Be my guests."

At that point Mrs. Shaw hooked her arm into Mrs. Norris'. "Why don't you young people go along without us? Mrs. Norris and I will have a nice quiet cup of tea somewhere, and a good talk."

It was arranged before Mrs. Norris could get the tacks off her tongue, Jimmie thought, but by the look on her face she was ready now to start spitting them. He leaned down and kissed her cheek. "Good night, dear mother of mine. Don't wait up for me."

Jimmie was not long in the company of these young ones before he felt his age, and furthermore, he knew they felt it. He did not intend to play-act much longer. He ordered their supper with an ease that impressed his guests; then he looked for a long moment at Miss Barbara Rossetti.

"You have a famous namesake," he said.

She cocked her head, contemplatively. "The poet, you mean?"

He nodded. "'My heart is like a singing bird.'"

She was a lovely girl, looking at him now, a disconcerting appreciation in her dark, deep eyes.

"The Yankees used to have a second baseman by that name," Arnold said. "Let's talk about him."

Jimmie turned a disbelieving eye upon him. "Do you like baseball?"

"I loathe it," Arnold said bluntly.

Jimmie smiled and folded his arms. "Then let's talk about Miss Daisy Thayer."

There was an instant's silence, stiff enough to have sat down amongst them.

"Brother," Arnold said then, "you know how to deliver a line, don't you? What about Daisy?"

"I suppose you might say I'm interested in anything you could call gossip."

"You're one of those columnists?" Miss Rossetti asked.

"God forbid! I'm a lawyer. I'm acting in the interests of a client of whom I think she is trying to take advantage."

"She's the girl who can do it," Arnold said. "She takes a man for everything he's got."

Jimmie could not ask the question on his tongue, not in present company. He turned to the girl. "She's a friend of yours, isn't she?"

"She was kind of a friend. We attended Stewart's personnel classes together. That's where I got to know her. And she did introduce me to Arnold afterwards..." She threw a worshipful glance his way.

Jimmie sighed after his own youth. "That was trusting of her, wasn't it?"

"She was through with me by then," Arnold said.

"And how did you feel about her?" Jimmie glanced at the girl. "You don't mind my asking him that, Barbara?"

She shook her head.

"I guess my vanity took it on the chin," Arnold admitted. "She's gorgeous looking."

Poor Teddy Adkins, Jimmie thought; his vanity had also taken it on the chin, and everyone would say it served him right, the bantam chasing after the bird of paradise. "I take it there's no doubt in either of your minds that Miss Thayer was out to find a man of money?"

"None," Arnold said.

"But there's nothing really wrong with that, is there? I mean nothing legally wrong with it," Barbara said.

"Quite right," Jimmie said. "It merely casts doubt on her moral integrity."

"And maybe she did fall in love with him," the girl added.

"Oh, come off it," Arnold said.

"I wonder if you're not talking about my client," Jimmie said, wanting her to say the name out of her own memory if possible.

"Someone by the name of Adkins?"

Jimmie nodded. He thought then what a fine appearance Barbara would make on the witness stand, and she would impress the women as well as the men: he would have that up on Daisy Thayer anyway. The problem was to get Barbara on the stand without hostility toward him.

"Perhaps we are misjudging Daisy," he allowed, since Miss Rossetti seemed to have a lingering confidence in Miss Thayer.

"I think you are," Barbara said. "I know a lot of good things she has done."

"Red Cross worker," Arnold said sarcastically.

"She worked very hard, too," Barbara snapped.

"Oh, sure, blood from stones *she* could get."

Jimmie was fascinated. His mind gave a leap to a happy conclusion: "Worked on the Blood Bank, didn't she?" he said.

"She got us over our quota, and nobody else seemed to care," Barbara said.

"She cheated," said Arnold. "Lined up all her bloody boobs like me and put us down as Mark Stewart's employees.

"I don't suppose the Bank records really care where the donors work," Jimmie said with an ease that belied his glee. "To them the only important information is blood type, isn't it?"

Barbara nodded, bless her innocence.

How Jimmie would have liked at that moment to ask the fatuous Arnold his blood type! But James Ransom Jarvis was a gentleman, and he cared not who had fathered Daisy's child. His only job was to exonerate little Teddy Adkins.

He smiled at Arnold. "Speaking of blood from a stone, what makes you think she was after Adkins' money?"

"Can you think of any other reason for her to check his credit the first time she met him?"

There was a bit of the mother in him, Jimmie thought. He had to tell everything he knew.

"I see what you mean," he said. "Did she do that?"

"Tell him, Babs."

Babs was not a blabber. "Wait till we have our drink," Jimmie said, seeing her reluctance, and himself satisfied to have got the conversation to a point of easy resumption. He talked then about the theatre of which he knew considerable, and admitted that occasionally he invested in it, aware of how favorable a light that placed him in. The "Irish Coffee" arrived, an excellent pickup for a nippy evening. Barbara's eyes shone with approval after her first taste.

"You were going to tell me about Daisy's checkup on my Mr. Adkins' credit," Jimmie prompted. "Let's get it over before our supper comes."

"I work in the Credit Department," Barbara started, "and

one day—it's over a year ago now—Daisy came up and asked me to look up the credit record on this man—she had the information off his charge plate, you see."

"His having purchased something from her," Jimmie said, trying to ease the revelation on.

"No," Barbara said tentatively. "I remember her saying she'd had to follow him all over the store to get it. Finally he'd bought something."

The cream aboard Jimmie's Irish Coffee seemed to curdle. "Why did she need the charge plate? Hadn't she just been to lunch with him?"

"Yes," Barbara said.

"I assume he introduced himself before inviting her," Jimmie said, but already suspecting his assumption had a false bottom.

"Oh, but he hadn't used his own name, you see," Barbara said brightly. "He'd told her a name like Cardova. Something like that."

It had been considerably less than frank of Mr. Theodore E. Adkins not to have confided the pseudonym to his lawyer, Jimmie thought. He might now prove Daisy to have tricked Mr. Adkins into paternity, but no jury could be outraged on behalf of a gentleman who did not use his own name on making overtures to the young lady.

23

Jasper Tully was not a man who liked to get out of New York City. In a town the size of Sando, Ohio, he felt lost. His feet could move round in his shoes. His coat left enough room between it and himself for the wind to crawl in and make free with his bones. Sando, at the hour of the milk train's arrival—and this was the only conveyance Tully had found out of Columbus—was gray with the sittings of coal-dust, and scarcely stirred at all at the sun's rising.

People came to New York from the damnedest places, Tully thought, and then did the most damnable things.

He inquired of the station master where the police department was. The man walked to the end of the platform with him in his shirt-sleeves, the sleeves puffed out around black elastic bands.

"Yonder," he said. "It's in the same building with the fire department. There ought to be somebody one place or other."

Tully arrived in time for the changing of the guard, as it were, the night man going off, and the day man coming on. He showed his identification. One of the men went into the back room from which came the smell of coffee. He returned with three cups and the pot. Tully had never had coffee he appreciated more.

"Who you looking for?" one of them asked then in the easy drawl of the hill country.

"A man by the name of Murdock, Edward T. Murdock."

The two policemen exchanged glances. "What'd he do?"

Tully assumed from their glances and from the size of the town that they knew the magician. "I want to question him in the murder of a couple of women."

"Murdock the Mighty?" the policeman said.

"What'd he do, saw 'em in two?" said the other.

It was fairly grisly humor, even for Sando, Tully thought. "Does he have any police record with you?"

"Might have. Licensing violation. He don't like having to pay to perform his magic shows."

"No felony record?"

"No-o-o. Why he couldn't put a dying rabbit out of misery."

"That kind's been known to have no trouble doing away with their wives, Joe," his partner said.

"But Murdock don't have a wife. Where's these women supposed to have been murdered?"

"They weren't *supposed* to be murdered, and they're not supposed to have been murdered," Tully said, concerned with semantics for once in his life. "They were both murdered in New York—one last week and one a couple of years ago."

"Took you quite a while to get round to that one, didn't it?" Joe drawled.

"Funny damn thing," his partner said, "we had a murder down here a while back. . .a Columbus doctor, what was his name. . .?"

Joe was thinking about Murdock, however: "Tell you, mister, I think you must have the wrong man. Murdock was out last week on what he calls his Cincinnati circuit, plays down one road, Washington Court House, Wilmington, Hamilton, and up the other, a show a night. I don't see how he could've been in New York when you said."

"To hang the truth up where the dogs can't get it," his partner chimed in, "I don't reckon Murdock ever has been to New York. Don't know anybody in Sando who has been lately, except old man Clinton. He owns the Number Two mine. It's the only one operating full shifts these days. You'll hear the morning toot blow any minute now."

Tully was ready to blow his own toot. "I think I'd better get to see Murdock just the same," he said, "and I'd appreciate it if one of you came with me."

Joe elected himself Tully's companion. The question was: would Murdock be home or was he out on the road again.

"If we don't find him, you can look up in the *Bugle* what circuit he's on," the Day Officer said.

Tully thanked him for the coffee, shook hands and followed Joe out of the station. The town had come awake since his arrival, and Joe knew everyone on the street. And everybody knew his companion for a stranger. Wherever Joe stopped—and he was not a man, going off duty, to miss his morning convivials—he introduced Tully as a friend of Murdock's.

That was just fine. It showed Joe to be a man of rare good sense. Tully liked him.

"If you have got the wrong man, no use harming poor old Murdock by telling everybody your business," Joe explained.

"No use at all," Tully agreed. If I got the wrong man, he thought, the gloomy prospect already explored by his subconscious.

The magician's truck, lettered MURDOCK THE MIGHTY, stood in the yard. That much luck he was going to have, Tully thought. Murdock himself, who apparently lived alone so far as human companionship, came to the door. As soon as he opened it, you could scent the company of livestock. Tully took a long deep look at the man. He was short and slight, hollow-cheeked and dark as a gypsy. He might even be an East Indian mystic, but he in no way resembled Johanson's fair, apple-cheeked boy who seemed also to have been Murdock's New York namesake.

"Is Murdock the name you were born with?" Tully said.

"It is."

"You're dark for an Irishman," the investigator commented.

"Not that I give a damn what a man is, as long as he is what he says he is."

The swarthy little man flashed him a beautiful smile. "I'm the great grandson of a tinker, or so I've been told."

"Are you?" said Tully. "Some of my mother's folks came from the west of Ireland. That's where most of the tinkers are, isn't it?"

"I've no idea," Murdock said.

"When was the last time you were in New York, Mr. Murdock?"

"1908, I think. That was the first, last and only time, Mr. Tully, and I don't remember it. I must have been four years old."

"Well, it's a long road that doesn't go anywhere," Tully said. "Would there be another man by your name belonging to the Society of Magicians?"

"Not till one of us died, sir. One at a time, and I've belonged to the Society for thirty years."

"Got any enemies you know of who'd go to some trouble to make mischief for you?"

"No," the magician said after some thought.

"Do you know anybody at all who might have gone to New York and taken your name while he was living there?"

The policeman Joe and Murdock looked at each other as though they thought Tully out of his senses.

"But somebody did it all the same," Tully said, "and furthermore gave as reference to your good name the president of the Society of Magicians."

"For God's sake," Murdock said.

"He registered at a hotel, joined a hospitality club, and furthermore, two years ago—and I'll give you the exact date in a minute—October 27, 1955, he let it be known that he was coming home. He bought a railway ticket for Sando, Ohio."

"Who is he then?" Joe asked.

"According to my records he's Edward T. Murdock."

For the first time, the magician looked as though he sensed trouble. Any man would, his identity borrowed, as Tully further remarked.

"Hey, this is bringing something back to me," Joe said. "You don't have a description of this man, do you?"

"I was coming to that," Tully said. He turned the page and read aloud the composite he had made from Johanson's and Reverend Blake's descriptions.

The magician shook his head when Tully was done, but Joe was sitting, his eyes blinking fast, his mouth slightly open. "Murdock, do you remember the Widow Bellowes?" he said then.

Murdock nodded.

The policeman turned to Tully. "We're going to have some ham and eggs. Then we're going up to the sheriff's office. It's three or four years ago, the Widow Bellowes—she was heir to the Bellowes' Coal Mines—got herself strangled to death and robbed of ten thousand dollars.

"She had this Columbus doctor coming to see her real often. Sometimes he stayed all night. Just a little scandal, not much. Sando is so far out of the way, most people got to stay all night when they get here. She had a big house, and everybody figured she could afford a fee to make it worth while for a city doctor to stay over.

"But here's the thing that'd curl your toenails—when the sheriff went up to question the Columbus doctor, he'd never heard of the Widow Bellowes." Joe shook his fist in the air. "The night the Widow Bellowes was strangled, the good doctor was seven hundred and fifty miles away, giving a lecture to ninety-five medical students in Des Moines, Iowa!"

Tully sat a moment in awed silence. One more murderer who had not been on the scene of the murder.

24

There was no doubt at all, Tully knew, reading the description of the man who had assumed the Columbus doctor's identity that it was Johanson's Jim-dandy. He had been slimmer, apparently, and wore a beard in those days. But the thing he had not disguised was his walk, his buoyant, cock-of-the-walk walk. Tully marveled at the audacity of the man to call attention to himself by wearing a beard in a town like Sando. Three days' stubble would not cause anyone to notice, but as the sheriff said, "This was a beard that would have pleasured General Grant."

"And the Widow Bellowes," Tully added.

"And her, and God knows, she was a hard woman to pleasure, wasn't she, Joe?"

The Sando policeman grinned. "I never tried it myself."

"Nobody would work for her, the way I heard it," the sheriff went on. "The house was filthy. People saw the 'doctor' hanging out things on the line himself. Whoever he was, he was a demon for cleanness. It must've been a real test for him to climb into bed with that woman."

"Had no trouble climbing out of it though," Tully said gloomily. "Out of it and out of Sando, and into New York City."

"Grand Central Station," Joe said. "Is it all as big as it sounds on the radio?"

"Bigger," Tully said. "And he got ten thousand dollars out of the widow. That's the money that must've taken him to New York in the first place. Or do you think he came here from there?"

The sheriff shrugged. "We traced him to Columbus. He just got on the eight o'clock train the morning after he'd murdered her and rode up there, neat, cheerful, like any man having business in the big town. And that's the last any of us or the Columbus police ever heard of him till now. Where he came from—well, he had a different kind of accent than any we're used to. Not much like yours either. Somebody said it was Oxford, England. Somebody else said Boston, and we took to that, him maybe being a Harvard medical man. You see we never did get it out of our heads he was a doctor."

"Did he treat anybody else while he was here?"

"Hey," Joe said, "we can get him for practicing without a medical degree."

"If that's all we can get him for," Tully said dryly. "I'm for seeing he gets the degree—honorary. How about it, anyone go up there with a busted finger or a bellyache, thinking him to be a doctor?"

There was no record of such an occurrence. Tully inquired then about the temper of Sando after the murder of a leading citizen, and by an outsider. The burden of the explanation was that Mrs. Bellowes had carried no favor with the local people. She had been known as a snob and as a cruel one, taking up at every chance with the outsiders. The town figured she got what she earned.

"The ten thousand dollars—did she keep amounts like that around the house, or was it got special out of the bank?"

"Two thousand was drawn out of the bank here just the day before. The rest out of banks in Columbus earlier. She was fixing to get married all right. She got her grandmother's wedding ring out of the safety vault, and a great black opal pendant. When you stop to think of them two things side by side, it'd give you the creeps, wouldn't it? Life in one and death in the other. The wedding ring was right on her bedroom table when they found her, but the black opal went east with him and the ten thousand dollars."

Tully sat back and thought a moment about Arabella Sperling's diamond pin, a "lover's knot," which was also missing. He told the two Ohio men about it.

"He must be getting quite a collection of female do-dabs," Joe said.

"Do-dabs hell," the sheriff said. "He's collecting the females, it looks like. How about that one with the pretty name, did she have any jewels?"

"Ellie True," Tully said. "That's exactly what I intend to find out first when I get back to New York."

25

Mr. Adkins arrived late Friday afternoon to pick up Jimmie and drive with him to Connecticut. He arrived considerably ahead of the hour he was expected by Jimmie. Indeed Jimmie had not yet come home from the office.

If there was a pattern shaping in these arrivals, Mrs. Norris no longer found it troublesome. She had more than half-expected him, and was dressed in her second best gown, a neat black silk, with delicate white lace at the throat and wrists. Her hair was parted in the middle as usual and disciplined into a bun at the back of her head.

"I suppose you've been told you resemble Queen Victoria," Adkins said, giving his overcoat into her arms.

"I've been told it, sir," she said.

He turned round and put out a firm hand to delay her way to the closet. "And what else have you been told, that you're 'sirring' me again? I thought we were democrats, you and I."

"I have no politics except Mr. James' when he's running."

"Nor I, even were Mr. James running. It was a social attitude of which I was speaking, and there, no matter how much of a snob you may be—and you are, you know—I am truly democratic."

"I have no trouble believing that," she said, and took his coat to the closet. "I was in Mark Stewart's yesterday."

"I see," Adkins said, and walked in his jaunty way to the study door. He might hang his head, Mrs. Norris thought, but he could not drag his feet. He was a cheerful man in spite of woe and weather.

He went into the study and lighted the lamp himself. In the room ahead of her, there was no need to play you-first, no-after-you at the door. "And I suppose you saw my former amour?" he said.

Mrs. Norris could not prevent the bob up her head gave at the word.

Nor was it lost by Mr. Adkins. He was hard put to suppress the pleasure it gave him to see her react to it. "Does the word offend you, my dear?"

"I suppose it did a mite," she said, aware of his "my dear." That had come out so offhandedly, it did not distress her.

"Since you were interested enough in my affairs to observe the woman," Adkins said quietly, "I thought you deserved the truth, however painful it might be for me to admit it. I did have strong feelings once for the woman."

"There are things in my own life it would be painful for me to admit," she said.

"I find that a solace," Adkins said. Then he looked up and smiled, rather like a small boy who had just been lectured and reprieved. "Do you suppose we might cadge—is that the word?—a glass of Mr. Jarvis' sherry?"

"The hospitality of the house is always mine to offer," Mrs. Norris said, and went to the wine cabinet.

"You will have a glass with me," Adkins said, and laid his hand on hers, but lightly, reassuringly, and surely with no undue intimacy.

"I prefer whiskey," Mrs. Norris said bluntly.

Adkins drew away in mock gravity. "Oh, my. I see what you mean about the painful admissions in your life."

They laughed together, and Mrs. Norris was persuaded to nip a bit of Scotch while he sipped his sherry.

"I suppose it is incomprehensible to you, how ever I could be attracted to a woman like Daisy Thayer," he said then.

Mrs. Norris would have preferred to forget that, but he, poor man, must be obsessed with it. "Oh, she's a woman of a certain beauty," she said.

"You have laid the truth in a bed of charity!" he cried. "Vanity. It was my vanity to which she appealed. Indeed that is the appeal such women make to all men. They are pied pipers, nay, to use your own word, dear Mrs. Norris, they are vipers. They sing to us, the long and the short of us, the fat and the hollow, and for a little while we think we are solid men."

It was an elegant sort of madness he was piping, a raving rhapsody all in the same key. At the end, Mrs. Norris said—having enjoyed both it and her whiskey—"You make such nice noise, Mr. Adkins."

He fairly rolled into a ball with pleasure. He grew grave then. "Why have you no faults, Mrs. Norris?"

"You're a peculiar sort of a man," she said thoughtfully, "who looks for the faults in an acquaintance."

"I've never had to look for them before," he said, and rubbed the knuckles of his hands with his thumbs as though there were an itch in them.

Mrs. Norris got up and brushed the crinkles out of her dress. "I don't suppose I have ever heard anything more conceited than that in my life...sir."

Mr. Adkins was genuinely shocked. He leapt to his feet. "Oh, my dear, you misunderstand. What kind of woman, but the wrong kind would care for an ugly little clown like myself?" He bobbed his head down to where the bald pate was shining in her face. "Look, I could paint a smile on the top of my head and who would know it from my face?"

"Oh, sir, that's a cruel thing to say of yourself. You have a very nice face. There's kindness in it, and sometimes a twinkle. It's true, it's not a handsome face, but I've always wondered how ever a handsome man could manage to be sincere. Except my Master Jamie, of course."

Mr. Adkins stood as though in bondage to her. He gave

his nose a wrinkle. "Don't be distracted with thoughts of him. Let me suppose for just one moment I am enough to fill your thoughts."

But he had lost her. She looked up at the clock, and at that moment the house phone gave a long and two short buzzes. "Now who would that be?" she said. "It is time for Mr. James, but he's in the habit of letting himself in."

She went to the hall phone, and behind her and not to her especial observance, Mr. Adkins took their glasses to the pantry. He did not care to have Jimmie know of their intimacy.

It was the doorman on the phone. "Your boss is on the way up, Mrs. Norris. I thought you might like to know it, you entertaining company."

Mrs. Norris fanned herself in a sudden wrath. "This not my company I'm entertaining, John."

"I'm glad to hear that. He's not my notion of company either." He hung up before Mrs. Norris could summon anything sufficiently scathing to say into the phone. The old goat had a mind like a rusty can.

Jimmie, meanwhile, was turning the key in the door. When he opened it, Adkins was the first person he saw, standing in the study doorway, his hands in his pockets.

"You're late," Adkins said.

"Sorry," said Jimmie, though he thought he was not all that late. He had never known a person of such punctuality. "How are you?" he said to Mrs. Norris, giving her his coat. "Perhaps you'll get Mr. Adkins a drink while I pack a few things."

"I'll bring you in one yourself, sir," she said.

"Good," said Jimmie.

She went to the kitchen for ice. Her face was so hot she would have liked to dip it into the ice bucket. And there when she turned around was Mr. Adkins standing and watching her, and with the strangest look—one almost of tenderness—seeming to try to tell her something with his eyes.

"Is there something, sir?"

"Sir," he mocked gently. He held her eyes with his own while he spoke. "I wish it were you and not your beloved Master Jamie with whom I were spending the week-end." He said the words in a sort of whispered despair, and left the room as soon as he had said them.

Really, Mrs. Norris thought, that was too bold of him. He should not have said anything like that even if he felt it. And for the life of her, she could not have said what she felt about him. It was not at all the comfortable sort of thing she felt for Jasper Tully. And yet there was pleasure in it.

They had but a moment alone after that. It was at the front door when Jimmie went back to his dressing room for something he had forgotten.

"Mrs. Norris," Mr. Adkins said, "stay at home tomorrow evening." It was just the shadow of a gesture, but she thought he touched his fingertips to his lips.

26

Jimmie felt like a snoop, and like one of the most vulgar sort, who, while enjoying the hospitality of your house, go about silently, eyeingly pricing the worth of everything, including your family relationships. But he had decided that if Teddy Adkins intended being less than frank with him, he was going to have to be the more informed on Teddy Adkins.

After dinner he had coffee and brandy with the immediate family: Mama, the three sisters and Teddy. Teddy, in their midst was entirely the person Jimmie had first supposed him, a cheerful nothing of a man, who, frankly, Jimmie doubted had ever slept with a woman, though Daisy Thayer might have coaxed him into her bedroom.

The sisters, one more than the other, doted on him. Although at least two of them had grown children and grandchildren, Teddy was still their baby brother. Miranda all but pinched his cheeks whenever she managed to get near him. Why? He was neither attractive nor admirable, at least that Jimmie could judge. Was it merely that he was something alive? Or was it that to them he was never altogether alive? He was like a doll. Yes, Jimmie mused, there was a doll-like quality about him, the band-box tailoring, the complexion, and above all that walk of his—like something with a tight spring.

The band-box, doll house atmosphere prevailed also in his rooms, Jimmie discovered later that evening when he stopped there on pretense of some small business. There were books in the cases, and clothes in the closet, but all of them had an undisturbed look, as though they might have been shifted on the hangers, the clothes, and the books might have been dusted, but none of them seemed worn. It was the damnedest thing, Jimmie thought, but he felt exactly the same way about Teddy Adkins: he simply was not worn enough for the years he was supposed to have been on this earth.

Jimmie went to his own room feeling more and more uneasy about the case and about his own presence in this house. He lay in bed thinking about it, a book open on his stomach—*The Life of Edward Coke*. If Elizabethan England could not distract him, what in God's name would? This house itself seemed unreal. Now and then a stirring of wind set the pine trees outside his window to a forlorn sighing. Poe must have heard such laments in nature to have written of the fall of Usher. And such a house might this be. Jimmie suddenly realized that he was doing precisely the old lady's bidding, and entirely against his own better judgment. This case should not be allowed to go to court. But the only reason he could give was scarcely valid: it was just bad taste! A gentleman could not tell a woman like Georgianna Adkins she had bad taste, damn it.

He was about to reach for a cigarette when a tapping came at his door. He looked at his watch. It was one in the morning. At six, the nephew Eric was to take him duck shooting.

"Yes?"

Miranda came in and closed the door behind herself before asking if it was all right. Her black, silver-shimmered hair was braided, and she wore a deep red corduroy housecoat that showed the extraordinarily feminine lines of her body. If this was woman at sixty, Jimmie thought, youth was a waste of time. He could not make up his mind to the proper behavior for himself. Should he leap up and get his dressing gown or roll over on his stomach and play dead?

Miranda came to the side of the bed and helped herself to one of his cigarettes. "Excuse the intrusion at this hour," she said. "But I saw that your light was on."

Jimmie motioned for a cigarette.

"I'm a grandmother," she said, smiling down at his articulateness. She held a match for him.

Jimmie inhaled deeply, and spiraled the smoke to the distance of his toes. "My housekeeper blows into my bedroom now and then," he said, "but whatever it is she wears on such occasions, she looks like a tea kettle. Forgive my manners. I should have got up."

"And offered me your bed?" she chided, and drew up a chair to the side of it.

"That doesn't sound decent, does it?" Jimmie murmured.

"Do you mind talking about Teddy?"

"Yes," Jimmie said, "I do. But that doesn't matter. I've done things I've minded more."

"It's surprising how little opportunity you and I would have to talk in the daytime." She put the ashtray on the edge of the bed where they both could reach it. "How does this whole affair, this suit, strike you, Mr. Jarvis?"

"It was only a couple of days ago," Jimmie said, "when you remarked that you did not intend to interfere."

"I did not intend to then, but I've come to think since that it has some rather sinister aspects. Since you don't want to talk, do you mind if I do?"

"I'm not a bad listener," he said, and smiled. It was truly a pleasure to look at her, the high cheek bones, the broad brow, the delicate mouth. By the looks of the women in this house, Teddy Adkins must have come into it from outer space in a basket, aye and perhaps between dropped off at some Shangri La for a century or two on the way.

Miranda studied her cigarette. "I don't think Daisy Thayer has very much to do with it at all. Has that ever occurred to you?"

"A lot of queer things about it have occurred to me," Jimmie admitted, "but that isn't one of them."

"I wonder," Miranda said, and her speculatives, fraught as they were with melodrama were making Jimmie distinctly nervous. He wished to God he was out of the bed and had some clothes on.

"Say out what's on your mind, Mrs. Thabor. It's after one o'clock and my wits are slow."

"Has it occurred to you that Teddy might be using this suit to break Mother's hold on his inheritance?"

"No," Jimmie said. "That did not occur to me."

"If this were not his intention—if it were something he wished to keep as much as possible from Mother's knowing—why did he not hire his own lawyer?"

"Because he was not prepared to pay for one," Jimmie said. "That's my opinion, if you're asking for one."

"I'm not. And I don't really care whether you concur in my views or not: but I believe Teddy is in collusion with Miss Daisy Thayer."

To hell with propriety, Jimmie thought. He kicked off the blankets and got out of bed and into robe and slippers. "You picked just the right person for your confidence, Mrs. Thabor," he said sarcastically, and trying hard to figure out why she had brought this choice monkey wrench to him. "I am trying hard to prepare an honorable defense for your brother, and in a case that will at best have many distasteful aspects. Distasteful that is to everyone, presumably, except your mother. She seems prepared to enjoy the victory whoever wins."

"That's exactly what I mean," Miranda cried. "And didn't Teddy know that would be her reaction, oh, didn't he know it! The wicked old witch. She cannot see that she and Teddy will break each other and scatter us all. She should be dead and in her grave. She would like to breed her family like livestock, and she has managed it with all of us—except the most important one with her. I do not believe for an instant that Teddy has a child..."

Just as had happened on their first acquaintance, Jimmie observed, Miranda the beautiful, the controlled, the articulate, became a jibbering fanatic on the subject of, or in the presence of, her brother.

"Do you have your brother's confidence?" Jimmie asked quietly.

"Certainly I do," she said, and squashed out her cigarette with determination.

"Then I wish you would go out from here now, Mrs. Thabor, and to his room. Tell him that you suspect him of collusion with Miss Daisy Thayer, and tell him that you've told it to his lawyer." Jimmie went to the door and opened it, and held it until she went from his room.

"You think I am afraid to do it, Mr. Jarvis. I am not."

"Good night," Jimmie said. This time he turned the key in his door. Sleep was even more elusive, and he tried lulling himself with the composition of a letter to his beloved friend in England. "Dearest," he started, "I am about to try a case which has involved me with the most primitive family, surely, this side of *Wuthering Heights*..." His reverie was interrupted by a woman's cry and within seconds, even while he sat stock upright trying to decide where it had come from, there was a shuffling and hurrying of footsteps in the hall. He waited. If anyone needed help, by the sound of the steps, plenty of people had turned out to give it.

Ten minutes passed, the commotion subsided, the whimpering voices faded, and Jimmie knew that he was not going to be called upon. He got up, into his gown and slippers and went out into the hall. He was just in time to see the butler go down the back stairs. Jimmie padded softly after the man.

He was within sight of the swinging door into the servants quarters when the man went through it, and he caught a glimpse of the young woman who waited him there. Jimmie hastened to catch their first exchange of words. It was a twist this, his spying at the servants' keyhole.

"You can go back to bed. It's all over," the man said.

"I can go back to New York in the morning, that's what I can do," the girl said. "There's lots of nice, respectable places, and with just as good wages. A man what throws mouthwash would just as soon pitch acid, I says."

"You says too much. I've worked for Mrs. Adkins for forty years, and I don't consider myself contaminated."

"Who would contaminate an old stick like you?" the girl said with a familiarity, Jimmie thought, that would have shocked Mrs. Norris.

"I was once a young buck," the butler said, "and all the kick isn't gone out of me yet. So button your nightgown before I'm tempted."

"EEEeh," the girl squealed, and Jimmie felt distinctly out of place. But within a few seconds, the girl asked: "Would you like a nice cup of tea, Mr. Timsey? It wouldn't take long. I've the kettle boiling."

Fortunately for Jimmie, Mr. Timsey accepted. Jimmie was again reminded of Mrs. Norris. She, too, wielded "a nice cup of tea" like a weapon.

The girl and Timsey settled near enough to the door for Jimmie to become their silent partner in the gossip.

"This fellow, Jarvis—the guest—he's a lawyer, you know. From what I could make out Lady Miranda had been in his room, and it put our Teddy in a fury."

"Is he a fairy?" the girl asked. Surely of Teddy, Jimmie thought.

"I don't really know. Forty years in the house, and I still can't make him out. But mark you this, young lady—stay away from him. There's nothing he likes better than to get a girl into trouble."

"That doesn't sound like one to me then," she said.

"I don't mean that kind of trouble," the butler said. "He has all kinds of mean tricks—like saying his pockets have been gone through. And he's done far worse. I remember a prune we had for a parlor maid—years ago this is—and he fixed her. One day when she was answering the upstairs calls, and he knew she was on all right, he asked her for his coffee. She went up with the tray and he opened the door to her stark naked. Pretended he thought it was me, to her that is. When I told Madam and she spoke to him, he said the woman had made it up. Furthermore, he said, she was always turning up in his room trying to surprise him. Madam discharged her on the spot."

"I'd have quit if I was her, but first I'd have let him have the hot coffee where he couldn't put clothes on for a while. That's dirty, what he did, Mr. Timsey."

"Exactly what I'm warning you, my girl. You'll get used to the eccentricities of old families. Like walking the deck on a rough sea it is. I can't help wondering though, what he's done now, with the lawyer here. Mind you now, you're not to repeat what I've told you to the other servants. You look to be a girl a man can speak his mind to, eh?"

"I don't like old families, Mr. Timsey. I'm going to apply for a position with a new one. A girl can say where she wants to work in times like these."

"With a new family," Timsey said scornfully, "you will be allowed to launder and do the Saturday scrubbing. They have no code, woman. In a house like ours a waitress has a trade, the upstairs maid is an artisan. Cooking and buttling are professions..."

Jimmie was about to retreat. He did not feel up to auditing a lecture on the domestic species at two in the morning.

"Besides, our Teddy isn't home often enough to give us much concern."

"I wondered about that," the girl said. "Sometimes his bed isn't slept in. I suppose a gentleman like him has a club he stays at?"

"That's what you're supposed to think," the butler said with a tone of finality. "Wash up the cups, my girl, or cook will scald the both of us at breakfast."

"She won't know it was us."

"Won't she now? She has a nose for midnight raiders."

Jimmie retired to his room. He had wondered himself at Adkins' lack of club affiliations. Not since his college days, apparently, had he joined anything.

If he was going to have to shoot ducks in the morning, Jimmie thought, he'd be shooting blind. But with a little more luck like tonight's he might at least know something of what he was about when it came to Daisy Thayer versus Teddy Adkins.

27

Tully got back to New York in time to have a good night's sleep in his own bed on Friday. He got up early, ate a hearty breakfast, and on his way downtown collected his thoughts from where his sister's palaver had scattered them.

At the office he called a meeting of himself, the investigator who had worked on the Ellie True case, and Lieutenant Greer, the Precinct officer in charge of the Sperling case. He called in also a couple of leg men.

"I hope you don't begrudge giving Saturday morning to chasing a Bluebeard, gentlemen."

"I'm a nature lover myself," the other man from his own office said.

"So he was a Bluebeard," Greer said.

"IS," said Tully. "Very much IS."

"Got a name for him yet?" said Greer.

"No, have you?" Tully snapped. Greer shook his head. Tully went on: "But what I have got may turn out to be a pretty good clue. Oh—I also have another murder to put down to his credit." He filled in the story from Sando, Ohio. "The pattern is similar. He uses the identity of a man, just picking it up like a pair of gloves, wearing it till he's done with it, and throwing it away."

"Like a shadow at night," Greer said.

"That's exactly right," Tully said. "But here's a taking-off point for us: remember Sperling's diamond pin?"

Greer's head shot up from his chest. "I've got something to say on that."

"Good," Tully said. "He seems to have taken a keepsake from the Widow Bellowes—a black opal pendant."

"A black opal," the other investigator said. "That rings a bell with me, Jasp..."

"I was hoping it would."

The Ellie True files were got out.

Lieutenant Greer said: "Want to hear my piece now?" He moistened his lips and Tully realized how excited he was. "I had Sperling's two nieces come in to see me yesterday. They had a confession to make. When they gave us the inventory okay on their aunt's jewelry, they didn't mention that one of the pieces was a stranger to them. They got a little greedy when they saw it. But finally their consciences got to working. They thought it might mean something to us."

"A black opal?" Tully ventured.

"Man, this is a ruby, ringed round by blue diamonds. I had it appraised last night; seven thousand dollars."

Tully sat a moment, his lips clamped on the speculation this started. Finally he said, "A piece like that must have a history. Did you put somebody on it?"

"I did."

Tully took an empty pipe from his desk; he pulled on it now and then, making a hollow sound. Every man in the room was thoughtful. His co-worker was still ploughing through the Ellie True files. Tully said: "Somehow, I can't imagine diamonds being friends with Ellie True. She was a working girl."

"That means there's another link missing then, doesn't it?" Greer said.

"At least one," Tully said grimly. "What else have your boys turned up?"

"Not much. We keep hammering away. The tenants upstairs of Sperling say now they sometimes thought she was crazy, laughing at the top of her lungs. They figured she had company though they didn't see him. He must be quite a jokester."

Tully nodded. "Like they say, you don't catch flies or women with vinegar."

His partner glanced up from the files. "You ought to know, Jasp."

Tully wagged a long finger at the man. "If you'd learned to read you wouldn't have such a hard time finding out what's in the files."

"Here it is, the property clerk's inventory—'one black opal, filigree gold chain. Presumed family heirloom.'"

"And where did you and the homicide boys think the True family loomed from?" Tully asked dryly.

The other investigator shuffled the files and answered what Tully had intended as merely a jibe. "Ellie True came up from Georgia. Poor white. She must've been the daughter of a Southern cracker."

"That's what I was digging at—did she have any money?"

"We never found out how much, Jasp. Not much, most people thought. No bank accounts. But she was close-fisted, saving to better herself for five years. Thought she could marry a millionaire, her having the Southern accent, her roommate said. And she was saving up for her trousseau. . ." The man was guiding his remarks by the testimony. "None of the savings ever showed up, so he must have got something out of her."

"His women seemed to have confidence in him, don't they?" Greer said.

Tully nodded. "He must set himself up as a man with money—temporarily short of funds. Nothing much new in that approach. But he must be a very capable faker. Smart, good with his hands—a doctor, a magician." He turned to the other man from the D.A.'s office. "Anything missing from Ellie True's jewel box?"

"That's what I'm looking for. Nothing listed. But that doesn't mean anything, Jasp. What she'd have of her own would probably not be worth listing, dime store junk."

"But something in it might've been worth taking for sentimental reasons," Tully said. "What's the name of her roommate?"

The man told him.

Tully made a note of it and the address and gave it to one of the leg men. "Here you go, Tommy. See if you can find her. Then find out if she remembers any jewelry of Ellie's at all, anything she especially liked to wear."

Tommy Bassett, a hard-working if not very imaginative youngster, was off.

"Suppose you do turn up such a piece, where will it get you?" Greer asked.

"To whoever it was he lifted the seven thousand dollar gem from, I hope. He must have climbed pretty high up on the social ladder for that one."

Tully addressed himself to the other leg man: "I want you to go through the records and report to me every woman who died a violent death in New York City in the past five years. Cause and circumstance. Case open or closed. I'm particularly interested in women with money now."

"Who isn't?" somebody quipped.

Tully asked Greer: "Could you get somebody from headquarters to tackle it from this angle: has any jewelry been lifted in the routine pickups?"

Tully himself went down to headquarters in the afternoon and went through the gallery. There was not a jolly face in the lot.

The first break came from Tommy Bassett: he called in that

he had found and talked with Ellie True's roommate. The only piece she could remember was a small gold "Florida leas." He spelled it when Tully asked him to.

Tully sat a time puzzling the word, saying it aloud. Suddenly it came to him: fleur-de-lis. "I don't know," he said. "They're getting educated men these days on the regular police force."

"But I went to college," Tommy protested.

"Come on in," Tully said. "You've done just fine."

His other man reported very late in the afternoon. There were a great number of known homicides of women during the period, one tenth of them open cases. Tully was almost through the open cases when he realized that it was dark outside. The office was deserted except for a cleaning man who was whistling something that sounded like *Saturday Night Is the Lonesomest Night of the Week*.

It was dinner time. He picked up the phone and called Mrs. Norris, asking her if she could by any chance join him.

"Thank you, Mr. Tully," she said, "but I already have an engagement."

"With a man?" Tully asked out before thinking.

"Does that surprise you?" she said.

Tully was too deep in the stream of his work to surface for a spinner. "Let me talk to Jimmie," he said.

"Mr. Jarvis is spending the week-end in Weston, Connecticut."

28

When Mrs. Norris hung up the phone, Mr. Adkins was standing beside her. "Mr. Tully," he said, "isn't that the young man you were telling me about, the detective?"

"It's been a long day since Jasper Tully was a young man," she said. "But that was him."

"You were a bit harsh on him, considering he was once your suitor."

"I wonder how that word came about," Mrs. Norris mused, "suitor. He wasn't that at all, Mr. Adkins, unless it means a comfortable kind of person to be with. In that way he suited me well enough."

Mr. Adkins made a mouth of disapproval. He was like a child at times. Then he would say things almost biblically wise.

"I hope," he said, "I am not becoming one of those comfortable people in your life."

Whatever he was, Mrs. Norris thought, he was certainly around a good bit. "Well, I am getting used to you, Mr. Adkins."

"Good God! That, my dear, is quite enough to drive a man such as myself to extremities. Used to me, indeed."

What, she wondered, was to him extreme. "You're a strange bundle," she said.

"That's better. I'd rather by far be strange than be an old shoe you could kick off in a corner. Comfortable, pah!" He put a finger beneath her chin. "Tell me the truth, are you really looking forward to a rocking chair by the fire and a slobbering old man to fetch you a cup of tea? Say yes to that and I'll go out the door."

"I'd as soon he wasn't slobbering," Mrs. Norris said, and her shoulders quivered with silent humor. Mr. Adkins laughed aloud.

"Oh, God bless! You are my kind of woman."

"That's a curry of nonsense," she said. "You said the same thing I'm sure to Miss Daisy Thayer, and God knows to how many before her."

"What?"

Mrs. Norris looked up at the sharp edge to his voice. He had gone quite pale. Oh, truly a strange little man. "Whenever a man fancies a woman, the woman he fancies is his kind of woman, or so he thinks at the moment. You know what they say—'I'll bet you tell that to all the girls.' That's all I meant, Mr. Adkins."

"No," he said quite severely. "I do not. 'All the girls,' as you call them, revolt me."

"I meant one at a time," she said. He had almost turned blue, like a baby in a pet, and him ordinarily a man with humor. "It was only a joke," she said.

"A disgusting one."

Mrs. Norris got up. "I don't know in what way I've offended you, sir, but I'm beginning to be a mite offended myself. I think it would be as well if you left now."

"No, no, no," Mr. Adkins protested, and paced away from her and then back again, the normal color gradually returning to his cheeks. He took her hand in his then—and his hands were quite cold, but strong. "Forgive me, dear one. I thought you were accusing me of...of promiscuity, and truly I am a very proper man."

"If you were not a gentleman, I should not have opened the door to you—on my own behalf, that is. But what a peculiar thing we're doing, talking this way! What interest could a man of your education and background find in a prickly bundle of gorse like myself?"

"I told you, my dear, I do not like comfort. A prickly bundle of gorse like yourself is much more to my liking than a velvet glove. I came tonight, wanting to talk of just that—of gorse and heather, lochs and leas, the leap of salmon and the burble of streams. I would like for my part to spend the second half of my life in the wilds of Scotland."

"The second half?"

"Oh, yes. I'm counting on the Scottish clime to double

my two score and fifteen. And do you know, my dear, I want double or nothing."

They soon eased again into conviviality. And in time Mr. Adkins mentioned that he understood Mr. Jarvis would marry soon.

"What did you say?" Mrs. Norris asked, not sure she had heard rightly.

"I don't have a document on it," Mr. Adkins said, "but it was my very clear understanding."

"And who will he marry?"

"I'm not that intimate with him, and it was not said to me. I merely overheard his remarks."

Mrs. Norris was caught between disbelief and hurt, for no intimation of such a thing had come to her since Mrs. Joyce had gone to England. "I will hear about it in sufficient time," she said.

"In sufficient time for what? You should think of it now, and I want you to. What I'm really suggesting, my dear—and I hope you won't think me shockingly bold—I want you to double your life with me. There! I've said it out. I don't want a word from you now. I know you're a woman of long independence, and probably of income sufficient to all the adventures of which you have dreamed.

"But I want to open to you a new world of adventure. Perhaps you know I shall be heir to an enormous fortune. More money—if we touched it—than you and I could count by dimes before the turn of the century. But I do not intend to touch it. When it is mine to give we will scatter it to a hundred thousand causes and perchance that way hit one that will grow good seed..."

She heard out his reverie, his nonsense rhyme, sitting tight with her own single thought like a dog with a bone in a crowded room. "Do I understand, Mr. Adkins," she said with quiet self-containment when he paused, "you are proposing that we go off to Scotland together and live another fifty-five years on *my* money?"

Mr. Adkins looked at her as though he were offended by so profane an interruption. "Are you so fond of money?"

"I'm fairly close with my own," she said, "and I can count it all by nickels, let alone by dimes, and while it won't have to do me till I'm a hundred and twenty-two—which is the age I'd be doubled—I don't intend to have to get by on the half of it, whatever the years left me."

"Ah, now," Mr. Adkins said, laughing, "how well you knew yourself to say you were a prickly bundle. Bless you, my dear, I have no intention of sharing your money. Rather I intend to match it, dollar for dollar, no more, no less. I'm an investment broker, woman. I'm bonded to at least twice your worth. That's why I offered my services to you the other day. I could advise your investment of money to return you a safe average of six percent. Are you making that now?"

"Three and a quarter," she admitted.

"The Bowery bank," he said with knowing deprecation. "What I should like to suggest—we match our small fortunes, mine to equal yours, and manage upon the income. Would you like to see my bond?"

"Your bond?"

"A certification of my right to invest—my brokerage license."

"I might," she said, "if I was going to consider your proposal."

"All I ask tonight," Mr. Adkins said, "and I beg it of you: do not insist upon answering my proposal now."

"Mr. Adkins, I don't like toting up a relationship this way."

"I could not agree with you more!" he cried, and bounded to her side. "But I know you to be a practical woman and I wanted you satisfied therein before I bespoke the night's true message. The night, as the song says, was made for love." And before she could take cognizance of his intentions he had plastered a wet kiss on her cheek.

She started up from the chair with such a bounce, she toppled her short-legged Romeo to the floor. He picked himself up with the most of a very little grace.

"I feel like something out of a Jane Austen novel," he said, "and I have never admired the only roles in that to which I was suited. You have hurt me deeply, Mrs. Norris. I am a sensitive man for all that I play the clown. There was something about you that seemed refreshing after my horrid experience with that, that wretch. You have disillusioned me terribly."

"I have hurt your pride," she said, "and what is pride to a man who has a sense of humor?"

His moment's contemplation of that seemed to mollify him.

"Yes," he said, "I am too sensitive, and I know I take

myself too seriously. My dear, your wisdom is the perfect balance to my wit."

He could persuade a bird, Mrs. Norris thought, to nest on a scramble egg. "I'm going to put on the kettle," she said, "and we'll have a nice cup of tea."

29

Jimmie had finally fallen so soundly asleep after his backstair wanderings, that he managed to be unwakeable at dawn Saturday. When he did get about the house, absolutely no reference was made to the nocturnal events of Friday. It was a dull, and for Jimmie, fruitless day and evening. Teddy's presence was so little felt, his absence was scarcely noted at dinner, Eric merely moving up to sit between his grandmother and mother. The one thing the boy managed from there was to persuade Jimmie to rise and shine at six A.M. on Sunday.

Jimmie had, he supposed, spent more miserable weekends, but he was hard put to remember one. It was bad enough to land in a wet duck blind before dawn of a raw November morning, but spending the next four hours in it with a decoy like Eric all but petrified him. He began to feel like something preserved in a jar. Every once in a while Eric would look round at him, presumably to see if he had turned blue. Otherwise there was no communication between them, or for that matter, between them and the ducks.

He was a handsome lad, Eric, being Miranda's son, and in his early twenties, and Jimmie wondered what he did besides hunt and fish. Did he make his own pocket money? Enough to take out the girls who must vie for his attentions. Or did they take him out? Nothing would surprise him about this family.

When they finally gave up the shoot for the day and got to coffee, Jimmie asked him what he did for a living.

"Oh, I expect to go in with Uncle Ted some day," Eric said. "He's not in a hurry to have me, and I'm in no rush for the 8:02 myself."

"Nobody in the family seems to be in a hurry," Jimmie said. "Is it a family concern—your uncle's brokerage?"

"No. It's something he invented himself," Eric said.

"That's a beautiful gun," Jimmie said, as Eric emptied the cartridges and began to oil the weapon. "Invented?"

"Sure. That office makes just enough money to support Grandma. We all know that. It's like his having a private printing press on which to run off exactly one thousand five-dollar bills."

"One might think he'd be tempted sometimes to increase the run," Jimmie said.

"Why?"

Jimmie shrugged. "Oh, just to break the monotony. Eric, if I were to ask you what was the nicest thing you could say about your uncle, what would it be?"

Eric thought about that. "I guess that he minds his own business," the boy said. "Everybody else in this family has a nose like an anteater, but Uncle Teddy, he just goes bouncing along with his in the air."

"You admire him then?"

"Not much," the boy said frankly. "He's a cornball."

"But you don't dislike him?"

"You mean on account of Mother, and the way she carries on over him?"

Jimmie nodded.

"You know my mother pretty well, don't you?" Eric said, and there was something sly in the way he said it that gave Jimmie a turn. He remembered the same sort of remark in the kitchen between Timsey and the girl.

"I've only met your mother twice," he said.

The boy curled one side of his mouth. "Then what was she doing in your room night before last?"

"Ant-eating," Jimmie said like a shot.

The neatness of the retort registered with Eric. "If I cared enough about my mother," he said, "maybe I'd be sore about the way she is over him. But if she carried on that way over me, I'd shoot her. Honest to God, I'd coax her out in the cattails along about twilight, ease off a ways from her and when the ducks flew high I'd shoot low."

"That's a nice, cold-blooded calculation," Jimmie said.

"Worked out well, too, isn't it? Uncle Ted says it won't work, not unless I can get her to fly up with the ducks."

"How did you know she was in my room?"

"Uncle Ted told me."

"Did he tell you why she was there—what she said to me?"

Eric shrugged.

"Just what did he tell you?" Jimmie persisted, suddenly expecting something important to hang by the answer.

The boy was ever so slightly embarrassed. But he tried to shrug that off, too. "He just said she was there, and called her a name."

"Like?" Jimmie tried with the monosyllable to keep the boy talking.

"A slut, that's all."

"A slut that's all," Jimmie repeated. "Where's your uncle now?"

"I guess he's still asleep if he came home last night."

"I thought you might have put him in the hospital for saying that about your mother," Jimmie said.

"Hell, it doesn't mean anything when Teddy says it, Mr. Jarvis. I don't even think he knows what it means."

"Then, since you seem to, shouldn't you assume the responsibility of teaching him?"

"No, sir. I like doing just what I do. I can see myself going on this way for fifty years, and Uncle Ted is the only person who can arrange that. I don't want to upset the status quo. Not me." Eric went to a bookshelf and disturbed the books in the only manner they had been disturbed for years, Jimmie thought: he had to move a couple of them to get a bottle out from behind them. "Like a little brandy in your coffee?"

"Yes," Jimmie said, "and a little more brandy than coffee, please."

30

There are people who would say that a man who works on the Sabbath does not deserve good fortune, and others who say that a man willing to work seven days a week deserves all the luck he can get. That Sunday morning, Jasper Tully, in a rare state of good cheer, just knew the breaks were due him.

He had before him what he called Bluebeard's Chart:

    Arabella Sperling
        Given: Ruby
        Gave up: Diamond lover's knot

? owned ruby
    Given what by killer? Gold fleur-de-lis?
Ellie True
    Given: Black opal
    Gave up: fleur-de-lis?
Widow Bellowes
    Given: nothing known
    Gave up: Black opal

Tully was determined for the moment at least not to go back beyond the Widow Bellowes. The two years between Ellie True's murder and Arabella Sperling's was the span on which now to concentrate. It broke down the file of violent deaths of New York women to something a bit easier to cope with. Somewhere in there was the woman who had owned the diamond-circled ruby—unless the killer had gone out of town again for that one. Tully didn't like to face up to that possibility. Thus far, although all the major insurance companies had been contacted, none had any record of its loss, or, even more to the point, of its existence. And that was just plain ridiculous, Tully thought.

Then came his first break of the day. Amongst the cache of property of questionable origin taken off recent law offenders and held by the police until ownership was established was a small gold pin, a fleur-de-lis. It had been taken from a petty thief, but seven-time offender called Buzzy Ritt.

Buzzy had gone straight for over a year, but this was promising to be a cold winter. Buzzy had just stolen an overcoat and three and a half pairs of gloves.

"Probably expected to have one hand chopped off for it, like in the old days," Tully said. "Where is he now?"

"In the Tombs," the leg man said.

"I'll just go down and brighten up his Sunday morning," Tully said, breathing thanks for his second break.

Buzzy took the occasion to spout his grievances against the city who couldn't bring him to trial any faster. It was all right for characters who could raise bail. They were out in the fresh air.

"I don't see what you're making such a fuss about," Tully said. "You only get homesick on the outside."

Buzzy made a vulgar noise.

"Buzzy, I understand the police are holding a little gold pin for you..."

"Yeah and I want it back. It belonged to my dear old mother."

"It's a valuable pin," Tully lied, but careful not to mention in what coinage.

"Huh?"

"Of course, a fence mightn't know that."

"I never had it to no fence," Buzzy said.

"I'll level with you," Tully said. "I want to know where you got that pin. I want to know badly."

"I told you. My mother gave it to me."

"When? It wasn't on you the last time you were up."

"I just didn't happen to have it along when I got picked up."

Actually Tully could not prove otherwise. He watched the thief carefully, but Buzzy Ritt had been in and out of too many tight places to show the pinch even when he felt it. Also, there was a chance that he was telling the truth. There must be a lot of gold pins in the world that shape. But if this one had any worth, Buzzy would long ago have parted with it—unless he was afraid to, unless he knew the pin was so hot that wherever it went, a murder rap went with it. In that case he would consider silence more golden than the pin.

"Okay, Buzzy, go back to sleep. I'm looking for a man and I thought you might help me."

"If you find him, bring him around. Maybe then I could help you out. Who knows?"

Tully weighed the remark. "I just might do that," he said.

A few minutes later he was studying the dossier on Charles "Buzzy" Ritt. At the time of Ellie True's murder, Buzzy was living in the west sixties. Two months later he moved to a two-bit hotel on the Bowery. He lived there for five months. A visit to the West Side Precinct yielded Tully nothing.

The Bowery hotel was different. Something had happened in there all right. And the date was right.

It was not murder by the record, but suicide, and one for which the police had been, most regretfully, grateful. It had occurred last New Year's Eve. Tully knew the story himself, roughly, but then, he knew a lot of stories, some rough, some smooth. The trouble was clearing the line to them in his memory.

On this one, he had the common police information—or, it might now turn out—misinformation.

For years before her suicide, Marjory Neville had been the

plague of the police. The daughter of a wealthy and politically influential family, she was poison from the age of twenty: drinking, whoring, even taking to dope. And always her offense had to be handled discreetly, delicately, and reported through channels. Then at times she would take to reform as violently as she had to debauchery. Her reforms ran to street preaching, public penance, all of which were as much of a plague to the police. But she could, till the end of her life, be counted on for trouble. She had fallen off the wagon the night she died.

No one was surprised at her last debauche—at least no one among the police whom she had kicked in the teeth. And there had seemed to be something natural, however obscene, in her taking the overdose in a Bowery hotel.

A regular genius of a public relationships man had taken over the press angle of the affair. Whatever went into the columns read like a dirge for a high-strung debutante.

Tully moistened his lips. The hush-hush of the press would suggest that an insurance hush-hush would have been a minor operation. And Buzzy had been living in the room opposite the debutante's!

If the little thief would talk, Tully thought, he would go bail for him himself.

31

Buzzy had just finished his dinner when Tully got back to him, and taking the cigar the detective offered him, he admitted he was feeling better about the city.

"Best meal I had since mother's cooking," Buzzy said, blowing a smoke ring that would have collared a horse. He was beginning to feel important.

"I always thought you were an orphan," Tully said. "That you had to make your own way in the world from the age of ten."

"That's a fact," Buzzy said. "I never got any breaks."

"A self made man," Tully said. "Ah, my lad, you've come a long way. You've mingled with high society and low, all kinds."

"A fact," Buzzy agreed.

"Remember Marjory Neville?" Tully drawled.

Buzzy choked on the smoke. "You're a snaky-tongued Mick, Tully, and your cigar's as rotten as your jokes." He dropped the cigar on the floor and put his foot on it.

"The D.A. gave me that," Tully said mournfully. "His own private blend."

Buzzy said what he thought it was made of.

"Okay, chum," Tully said, "I got a man I want to talk to you about. You got a little gold plated pin not worth two bucks. Maybe you took it from her alive, maybe dead. It doesn't mean that to me." Tully snapped his fingers. "The lad I'm after took a piece of jewelry from her worth seven thousand dollars. Doesn't that make you feel like a midget? And I'm pretty sure it was him gave her that little gold flower you're carrying around since. Know where he got it?"

Buzzy only stared. He wasn't talking yet, but he was interested.

"He took it from Ellie True. Remember her? The minister was tried for her murder..."

Buzzy wagged his head in recollection.

"It begins now to look like the Neville woman didn't take all those powders on purpose," Tully went on like a purring cat, "and if she didn't, it means she was Number Three on my man's list of what we could call...extinguished females. He ticked off Number Four last week. See why I don't care how you got the pin? I just want to know where, and what you know about what happened to Miss Neville."

Buzzy opened up. "Want to know something? I think the Neville dame was mixed up with a minister, too."

Tully grinned. "Buzzy, you're a gentleman."

"She had this soup kitchen on the Bowery," the prisoner started. "It was a kind of mission house, and this little guy—the damnedest looking little red-headed, red bearded—he wore one of them Van Dykes, you know what comes to a point?"

"I know what comes to a point," Tully said, fascinated in spite of himself.

"Well, he did the preaching. I used to go round for the eats. The minister, he talked just like her, all beautiful words, but no sense, see? But he was hell-fire good on the singing and most of the nuts around like that. I don't have a ear for music myself. Well, this went on a couple of months maybe. The grub—like it was catered. I went regular. And she was real serious about the mission. We all knew it was her had the money, and I heard from somebody she was a reformed drunk. The needle too. But she figured she was going to make up for all her sins, hiring us a salvation preacher."

"The preacher," Tully said, rubbing his pipe affectionately, "tell me some more about him."

"What's to tell? He had the gift of gab, that's all, and what I could make out, the only thing wrong with the world was women. Who listened to him after that? Me, I like women just fine."

"What did he look like?" Tully persisted. "Suppose he was

coming down that corridor—how far would he be before you'd recognize him?"

"With that walk of his? I could tell him coming round the corner. Like a bouncing ball."

"That's my boy," Tully said affectionately.

"You want to know about the night she passed out," Buzzy went on, and Tully knew now where he had got his nickname. Once he started talking, he could buzz.

Tully nodded.

"We didn't know her by the name of Neville, of course. That come out after the police was there, and she was identified. All we knew, she was 'Sister Marge.' I thought she was whacky at first, see, just plain off her track, but I got used to her. Then that night she comes flipping into my room like she had wings. 'Buzzy,' she says, 'wish me the joy of the morning, for I'm to be married tomorrow.' So I wished her. That was maybe ten o'clock. By eleven she was singing hymns, but it didn't sound like religion to me, and I was getting thirsty. I figured all that singing just had to come out of a bottle. And I was right. I went over and interrupted them. It was the Reverend Preacher opened the door.

"I stuck my hand out to him and says, 'Congratulations.' 'For what?' he says and I ask him: 'Aren't you the bridegroom-to-be?' 'Certainly not,' he says. And cold sober. He said something about her being beyond his help and walked out. So there we were, her and me, with three quarters a bottle of whiskey. I poured us drinks. We clicked glasses, and I said: 'To the bride.' But she was already falling asleep."

It might have been at that moment, Tully thought, that Buzzy acquired the gold pin. It wasn't worth mentioning now. "The drink you poured her, was it in a clean glass?"

"No. The cops asked me that. I just added a good hooker to what she already had in the glass. As long as she was nodding, I took the bottle home with me. It turned out she woke up. Maybe she looked for a drink. I felt bad about that. She must've been feeling mighty low to do what she did."

"If she did it," Tully said. "Three quarters of the bottle left when you got there. Do you suppose she had another bottle?"

"No empties. The cops looked."

"What was the preacher's name?"

"I've been trying to remember—Drake, Buck—something easy."

"Not Blake?" Tully said, incredulous.

"No. It wasn't just that."

"You didn't see him again, I suppose."

"Only at the station. But I tell you, I cleared out myself as soon as the cops let go of me."

"Didn't the police frisk you, Buzzy?"

"Nope, and I've been thinking about it since you mentioned that expensive jewel. Why didn't they?"

"I'll ask them that myself," Tully said, getting up. "But I think I know the answer. They didn't know it was missing." At the door while he signaled the guard that he was through talking to the prisoner, he said: "Do you want bail posted, Buzzy? I know a man who'd do it for me."

The man thought about it. "What's the weather like?"

"Cold as a witch's kiss."

Buzzy settled back in the chair, his hands behind his head. "I just think I'll let nature take its course."

Tully got back to his office in a hurry. It was almost as hard to get information about the Neville "suicide" from police circles as it would be from her family. Her death had come at the time her father had just been confirmed in an important ambassador's post. The family home was in Norwalk, Connecticut.

Tully called the Chief Medical Examiner himself. Meanwhile he had Tommy Bassett call Mrs. Norris and get from her information on where Jimmie could be reached. Weston was within ten miles of Norwalk, and Jimmie was discreet, persuasive, had the D.A.'s office behind him, and was himself high born enough for the Nevilles to talk to—if they would talk to anyone.

Being a quick and efficient lad, so far as his brains took him, Bassett got Jimmie on the phone before giving it to Tully. Tully briefed Jimmie on the information he wanted: what the family knew, if anything, about the preacher, and the story on the jewel. He could play a melancholy tune to them—their daughter had not taken her own life likely, however willing they had been to accept that verdict.

Tully went then to see the Precinct Captain of the district wherein the suicide had occurred. It hadn't taken them long to clean up the case at the time.

"Do you mean to say you didn't even bring in the so-called missionary?"

"Godalmighty, the problem wasn't bringing him in," the captain exploded. "The problem was getting him out. He was in here every day for a week, volunteering this and that—nosing around to see if she left his mission something. Finally, we told him to go see the old man.

"That, he thought, was a good idea. The family might set up a memorial fund for the mission. That's how we got him out of our hair."

Tully shook his head. "Oh, the arrogant pup!"

32

While the prospect of the job he had agreed to do for Tully was not especially pleasant, Jimmie was glad of the diversion from the Adkins family. He had spent most of the day in their library of uncut books. Miranda had not spoken to him again. Teddy had cured her, apparently, of intimacies on his behalf. Teddy himself had disappeared after cocktails on Saturday night and had not been seen since. He was in the habit of doing that, his mother said, the family being too much for him. Jimmie had no trouble understanding that much about Teddy Adkins.

There was something very wonderful about Connecticut roads in late November, a brown and gray landscape that caught and held any chance bit of color as though waiting for the artist who would come and put it to canvas. And, alas, there was not much left of that part of the state that had not been put to canvas or to house or to antique shoppe...unless it was the few grand estates remaining.

Turning into the long poplared drive of the Neville estate, Jimmie wondered how the household would stand comparison with that which he had just left. He could remember having met Marjory Neville on a few occasions in the forties, a wild sort of girl then with an angular beauty that must have died a horrible death in her dissipation. He had not seen her for at least five years before her death. He recalled now, Helene Joyce had once remarked that Marjory Neville had a wonderful face to sculpt. And he could remember what Helene had said when she died: She had used and misused life for thirty-five years. Then she wrapped it up in an old rag and threw it away.

Later, having got Andrew Neville to the point where he would talk of his daughter even though it grieved him, Jimmie thought again of Helene's remark when the old man said: "If only she had died a clean death."

Jimmie could almost feel the weight of years that had come upon Neville in the wake of the tragedy. He had withdrawn from public life, indeed even from the company of intimate friends.

"I've been told, sir, that she completely rehabilitated herself. That takes a great deal of strength."

"Without a great deal of strength she could not have persevered in so much debauchery," the man said bitterly. "Oh, I am being less than honest, Jarvis. What turned my soul to acid, she deceived me at the end. I believed she was sincere. I believed her cured. I did not approve her mad venture of saving all the derelicts on the Bowery. And where she lived revolted me. But she had turned a dismal hotel room into a nun's cell: scrubbed and bare, austere as charity..."

"You were there?"

The old man nodded. "She had caught me up with that child-like joy. She always could. And she had such faith in this young missionary."

"Did you get to know him?"

Neville shook his head. "She had intended that I meet him, but he had gone on a begging expedition on that occasion—that's what she called it."

Jimmie hated to put this question, but no better time for it was likely to come: "Did you contribute to the mission, Mr. Neville?"

"Five thousand dollars. I had wanted to meet the young man first. But knowing the other men with whom she had at one time or other been involved, I was too well satisfied in merely knowing his profession."

"What did she tell you about him?"

Andrew Neville drew his long fingers down his gaunt cheeks until he much resembled an El Greco painting. "That he was not handsome, but that he was pure. She had got an obsession on purity, you see."

"Anything about where he had come from?"

"She said, I believe, that his family background was similar to hers. He came from San Francisco."

"And his name?"

"Francis Drake. Not easily forgotten."

Jimmie agreed. "A pirate, wasn't he, on what might be called a continental level?"

"Yes," the old man said.

"What about the gem, the ruby, Mr. Neville?"

The old man started up violently, and one of the corners of his mouth twitched. He had had a stroke recently, Jimmie thought. "It was some time later I discovered that was missing," he said finally. "I did not want the affair revived. My lawyers had already paid heavily to have the tragedy quietly forgotten. I had the brooch removed from the insurance inventory."

"You may be able to recover it now," Jimmie said.

"I shall consider it a breach of faith if you suggest it, Jarvis. I have been painfully frank with you upon your promise of confidence."

"Would you release me from that promise if it becomes evident that Marjory Neville did not commit suicide? That she was likely persuaded to take one drink to toast an engagement to marry this preacher, that she didn't drink much at all that night, but was probably drugged?"

The old man covered his eyes with trembling fingers. "By him?"

"Yes," Jimmie said. "She was likely murdered, and if at the time you had not been so willing to believe her beyond rescue, and so zealous of your own good name. . ."

"My own good name," Neville interrupted, "my ambition, my fortune, my life—all of them are crumbled like dry leaves.

Look at me. All there is left of me is yours to put on public exhibit—if you can prove that."

"Thank you," Jimmie said, and got up. "Please don't disturb yourself. I shall go out by the garden. I expect a gentleman from the New York District Attorney's office will come to see you when he needs your cooperation. He is a good man, Jasper Tully."

Andrew Neville merely nodded. Glancing back at him, huddled as he was in a great leather chair, Jimmie thought he looked like something which had tumbled there from among the curios lining the walls of this, his trophy room.

Jimmie called Tully from a public phone booth.

"So he got five thousand dollars, and a ruby he gave to a scrub-girl," Tully said in summary. "What was the name he used?"

"Francis Drake. . .like Queen Elizabeth's boy. And he came from San Francisco, so he told her, from a family like her own."

"A little truth, a little fancy," Tully said. "I'm obliged to you, Jimmie. Come in the office when you can and take a look at the whole picture. It's going to be one of the damnedest cases ever brought to trial—if we get the wily bastard."

"You will," Jimmie said. "Tully always gets his man."

"But never his woman," Tully cracked.

"I was wondering what happened between you and Mrs. Norris," Jimmie said.

"You'd better ask her. I think she's got another boy friend."

"That will be the day," Jimmie said.

33

As Jimmie drove back to the Adkins estate, he had ample opportunity to contemplate the modern condition of two ancient fortunes. Despite their obvious differences, the Adkins house and Neville's had at least an atmosphere in common: decay was well set in in both instances—the old man dying alone, and the very old woman surrounded by decadent offspring. There was a deadly torpor among them all—except for old Georgianna Adkins and her son. In them a little torpor might have been desirable!

Just how, Jimmie wondered, was he ever going to persuade his senior partner that it would be a very fortunate day if they got out of court without raking through a veritable pit of disease. Jimmie now believed from incident, kitchen rumor and Eric that Teddy Adkins was far from what current society called "normal." Nor was he Milquetoast or Casanova, either of which would have been defensible. Seeing him walk in that peculiar, light-footed way of his one might suspect now, Jimmie mused, that he had come by it from trying to stretch high enough to peep into windows. That was the feeling Jimmie was getting about him, and it was not good.

Jimmie drew a long and refreshing breath through the open car window. He had thought after his morning for ducks he would never enjoy fresh air again. Whether to have another go at Mama—that was the question. Could he possibly persuade her to settle out of court? Did he dare to prophesy that instead of winning either way, Mama was likely to lose either way? He might force Miss Daisy Thayer to the point where she would admit Teddy Adkins was not the father of her child—but if she had a mind to tell it—what did she have on the little dandy that she dared bring him into court on false charges? She had known a bad thing when she saw it, and she had known what it might be good for.

All in all, the week-end was not lost, considering the purpose for which he had come, Jimmie decided. He knew at least the slough through which he must wade and try to come out alive.

An ironic thought then struck him: he had abandoned

politics to practice law and amongst the noblest of its advocates, a firm which would not touch divorce lest it compromise its proud tides!

Teddy Adkins was standing in the driveway when Jimmie drove up. He wore a scarf around his neck, its ends flying to the winds, and his bald head as ruddy in the frosty wind as his cheeks. He looked full of health and vigor—exuberant as a Dickensian hero. What a shame it was, Jimmie thought, to have to crack this apple open, and it so beautiful just to look at!

"You'll have Sunday dinner with us before returning to town," Adkins said. "We have just time for a drink before it's gonged out to us."

"You look in fine fettle," Jimmie said.

"Oh, I am, I am," Adkins said. "I'm sorry to have abandoned you, Jarvis, but I may say now I had a matter of courting to attend."

"Courting?" Jimmie repeated, wondering if he had heard rightly.

"Oh, yes," said Teddy blithely. "And I have every reason to be confident in the success of my suit."

"You'd better attend one suit before pressing another," Jimmie said dryly.

"Ah, dear man, this time all is different. I have found a woman with whom I can be myself, whom I shall persuade to love me for my own sweet sake."

Poetic anyway, Jimmie thought. And all his calculations of the man were going a-kilter again. He swore to himself and wished profoundly that Tully's mission had not delayed his departure from Connecticut. If he had left soon enough he would have gone out on a straight line at least. "You don't seem to have any trouble finding them," he said.

"The women?" Adkins threw back his head and laughed with the grotesque glee of a mad child. He wiped his eyes. "An exaggeration that, of course, dear man, but a flattering one." His sister Miranda met them at the door. Teddy took her arm. "Mr. Jarvis has just paid me an outrageous compliment," he said.

They went in to where the rest of the clan were gathered for the daily ritual of sherry or madeira in the great parlor which, Jimmie noticed, smelled of dogs and woodsmoke—the most masculine thing about the place.

"Mr. Jarvis and I will have whiskey, Timsey." Adkins turned to Jimmie. "You prefer Scotch, don't you?"

Jimmie nodded, watching Timsey.

Timsey said: "Whiskey?" and let his eyes run along the floor to Mama's feet and up then to her face. Having found acquiescence there to Teddy's wish, he said, "Yes, sir," with sublime submission.

The whiskey, Jimmie suspected when it did arrive, had been watered. He would like someday to pick Timsey's mind, he thought, if he could find anything small enough to pick it with.

Jimmie lifted his glass and toasted with abandon: "To victory with honor."

"To our own dear Teddy," Miranda said sickeningly.

Teddy turned on her. "You had better swaddle your own son, Mandy." He pushed his chubby face into hers. "Teddy is going to run away from home."

"Hear! Hear!" the old lady cried.

Miranda whirled about on her mother. "Why didn't you wean him as a child then? You're trying to thrust him out in the world now, to harden him up like—like something or other before you die."

Miranda's outburst dried up, and the whole room seemed brittle with age and dust, as though any words loosed in it would themselves fragment and disintegrate.

"That, my dear sister," Teddy said, "is a very apt description of me—a something or other."

Mercifully, Timsey came round then with the gong, running hard upon the service of whiskey, Jimmie thought.

Teddy took his accustomed place at the table after seating his mother, but there the pattern broke. He poked and probed and titillated almost everyone at the table, even those whose names or relationships to himself he scarcely knew, Jimmie thought. He was, in fact, a new man.

"Do you know, dear Jarvis, my nephew, Eric, is going to apprentice to me? And I think we shall both start over in that case. I don't suppose I've told you how I came to be a broker, an amusing little tale which I trust the family will forgive my repeating again in their presence. I began with the alphabet—artist, abattoir—oh, yes—I considered everything that came to mind in the 'a's, and nothing there seemed quite suited to my disposition. So I came to the 'b's. . ."

It should have been the birds and the bees, Jimmie thought.

"But now, as I say, we shall start over. I have discovered an 'a' I'd forgot. Alchemy. How does that suit you, Eric, my lad? Alchemy and black magic."

"Just fine, uncle," Eric said, frolicsome as a toad.

"Isn't he a splendid chap?" Teddy said.

After dinner, and when all his adieus had been said to the elder family, Jimmie sought out Eric in the gun room. He practiced the hypocrisy of thanking him for the duck shoot. "Your uncle came back in high spirits, didn't he?"

"Didn't you ever see him that way before?"

"No," Jimmie said. "Does it happen often?"

"Once in a while. Like a talking jag."

"How long does it last?"

"Oh, a day or two. It sure livens up things around here while it lasts."

"Then what happens?"

"He goes off on a trip somewhere, and when he comes back, well, we're all right back where we started before the merry-go-round went round."

"You're an extraordinary family," Jimmie said, and offered his hand by way of getting away. "Thanks again, Eric."

"Never met one like us before, did you?"

"There can't be many," Jimmie said.

"Well, that's the way the ball bounces," Eric said.

Jimmie could not get the bloody phrase out of his mind all the way home although, God knows, he had other things to think about.

34

Tully studied the intervals at which the known murders had occurred. He wondered if the time for killing was by any chance, set by the man's need for money. He had got five thousand dollars from two of the women, ten from one, and probably every cent Ellie True had. There had been at least a year between all of them which indicated some margin of present safety. But who dared predict that? It was fine for the psychiatrists to prognosticate. A detective didn't care.

The investigator was convinced they could catch the man now by his very arrogance, his determination to follow a pattern, his confidence in his own superiority to the law, the common intelligence, and above all to the women whom he bilked and murdered. He was versatile in that, the clever villain: he knew wherein not to set patterns. But in the end, Tully thought, it would be a little thing that would trick and tumble him.

What had taken him out of New York on that one known occasion?

Why Sando?

He had assumed a doctor's identity there, and while there, he had watched a magic show of Murdock's or had been in some way associated with the magician. It still didn't answer the question: Why Sando?

Tully went over the notes he had made in the Ohio town. He had a notation on *The Sando Bugle*. The night officer of the police had said he could find Murdock's itinerary there if the magician was not at home. That itinerary must have been very important to the murderer during the last days of Ellie True.

Tully had more confidence in the New York Public Library than he had in himself. He called the reference desk. The librarian he spoke to thought it unlikely they should have *The Sando Bugle,* but he checked. It was with almost personal pride that he returned to say that the Newspaper Annex had two one-year files of the paper. But the annex was closed on Sunday.

"I can wait till morning," Tully said, but he could feel a pulse of excitement. The files—with a year's lapse between them—covered the periods of the Bellowes murder and the murder of Ellie True. "How do you suppose the library comes to have those files?" he asked.

"Likely a gift subscription. Or a request to subscribe with a very good reason."

Tully had no doubt it was a gift subscription, and a very good reason was no doubt given for the keeping of them—in the name of a mining engineer, or a professor of metallurgy.

Tully next put in a call to Joe, his friend on the Sando force, and asked him to check with the circulation department of *The Bugle*. How had they got the subscription from the New York Public Library?

Joe called back within an hour. A cash transaction, the first subscription, across the counter. The second one had probably come through the mail, but cash, too.

"Tell you what was going on down here at the time might've interested your Wall Street people—some gold mining outfit was taking over control of the Bellowes mines, and all the other coal mines it could buy in. There was a whole anti-trust business blew up over it."

Tully didn't say so but he could not see Wall Street going to *The Sando Bugle* for its information. He said: "But why have the paper sent to the Public Library?"

"Maybe the light's better there," Joe said. "I know that's the case down here. Best light in town's in our library."

Tully thought of all the lights in lower Manhattan. "I wish we could say the same," he said. "Thanks, Joe."

He sat then and mused on whether perhaps the killer was going to turn up next in the disguise of a mining engineer, or perhaps a business tycoon.

That gave him pause. They did not know yet what guise

he had taken in his courtship of Arabella Sperling. She had spoken of her "broker's" advice. Tully went back to Johanson's testimony. The man he had seen leaving her house carried a brief case and umbrella.

Tully put the phone on night service and went home. He wanted to start fresh in the morning, to move the more surely, directly.

There was yet another role for the murderer to play, and this it was that gave the issue urgency. The moment was surely coming when the man's mad ego would require that he take the ultimate risk. The day he decided to play himself, they could throw away any timetable his previous crimes suggested.

35

Mrs. Norris told herself over and over throughout the day that she would not go to meet him. It was safe to admit she was infatuated, though never in her life before had that word had any place in it. She was daft to even think of seeing him, much less of marrying him, and she was not at all sure he wasn't himself off to have asked her. He bubbled up like a pot on the stove, popping its lid though it wasn't half full.

But she liked the music of it: there was no denying that. She could remember to this day her mother's counsel: "No woman, whether sixteen or sixty can afford to turn her back on an honest proposal of matrimony—unless she already has one in writing."

She was dressed in her best navy blue when Jimmie arrived home from Connecticut.

"I've had dinner," he said in a fairly somber mood, "so don't let me delay you."

"Was it a pleasant week-end?"

"Jolly."

"Have you heard from England lately," Mrs. Norris inquired, "from your nice Mrs. Joyce?"

Jimmie scowled at her as though he expected her next to ask for an exorbitant raise. "I'm thinking of closing up the house and joining her," he said threateningly.

Mrs. Norris ruffled her shoulders. "You might at least give a person sufficient notice."

Jimmie threw up his hands in disgust. "Oh, for God's sake," he said, and ploughed into the study, closing the door behind him.

Mrs. Norris met Mr. Adkins in a quiet corner of the Tavern on the Green in Central Park. He was dressed in a dark suit and with the white cuffs of his shirt gleaming. Nothing so impressed Mrs. Norris in a man's dress as just the right amount of snowy cuff slipping casually out of his sleeve—unless it was as white a bit of undershirt showing at an open collar. Of one thing she might be sure about Mr. Adkins: his linens would be impeccable. And things like that did give a woman a sense of pride in a man.

The tavern was not crowded at that hour, and unperceived by any eye which might disparage the gesture, Mr. Adkins took her gloved hand in his and in just an instant brushed it with his lips. To have gainsaid him that would have been to make more of the incident than it merited. He was merely being his flamboyant self. He had said himself he counted on her Scottish caution to settle him.

Mrs. Norris wished to heaven she could settle him—or herself. Her heart was thumping like a Waterbury clock.

"Oh, my dear, you look stunning!" he cried. "Blue, isn't it? The gods be praised you've thrown off the widow's black."

"I'll be throwing it on again tomorrow," she said. "It's still middling new."

Mr. Adkins drew two leather chairs to the windows. They were edged with steam, the windows, but through the center of the many panes, the whole of a neon twilight shone. "I thought we might have our drink here," he said, "then our dinner where there's music. There's so much I have to discover of you: do you dance?"

"Nought but the fling," she said with a wink.

Mr. Adkins cleared his throat. "I certainly shan't tempt you into that tonight. Or perhaps I shall!"

He went off then and brought their drinks himself. Mrs. Norris prayed hers would sober her. She was not at all steady without it.

"'I went into a public 'ouse to get a pint o' beer,'" he quipped. "Remember that? Rudyard Kipling's man, Tommy Adkins."

"Any relation?" Mrs. Norris said.

"I shouldn't be at all surprised. I come of very simple origins."

"Isn't it strange," Mrs. Norris said, folding her hands round the empty glass, "here am I, the great-great-great-granddaughter of a Scottish chieftain, and keeping house for a barrister."

"There's a very natural answer to that," Mr. Adkins eased in. "Hereafter you will keep house *with* an ex-stockbroker, a house and a garden and a small fire in the grate. And I'll be the one to bar the door! Do you have a passport?"

"I do, but..."

"But-me-not. Rather, hear me through." He took from his breast pocket a picture of a matched cottage, the roses tumbling around it, a river bending into the distance. "All this can be yours, my dear. This is the beloved bit of Scotland I have chosen to present you."

"There are no thatches in Scotland that I know," she said.

"That is why I chose this house!" he cried. "I wanted for you all the virtues of your native land, and a little bit more, something different. When we get there we can change it."

We can change it before we get there, Mrs. Norris thought, and drew in a deep breath she let out in a sigh. The time had come to put an end to his golden dream-talk. "Mr. Adkins..."

"Sh-sh... Your sigh is a thrill to me, more eloquent far than words."

She leaned over to look more closely at him. She could not believe it: there were tears in his eyes. He did believe what he was saying! He thought he had persuaded her.

"Oh, my goodness," she said. "Thank you, Mr. Adkins..."

He was shaking his head like a mop. "Wait," he said, a catch in his voice. "Will you wait?" He took a handkerchief from his pocket.

"Yes," she said, presuming to wait for him to blow his nose.

"Forever?" he said.

"For what?" said she.

"Then for a day only. Tomorrow, we shall seal our bargain. Tonight is merely the pledge of our hearts. Tonight, my dear, you shall take home with you a lover's knot." He opened the handkerchief and plucked from it a small glittering bow of diamonds.

Mrs. Norris could only say, "Oh."

Mr. Adkins placed the tiny jeweled bow on the dark blue sleeve where she could better see it. It glittered like something wet and crawling.

"Put it away," she managed. "It's too beautiful for the likes of me. Oh, truly Mr. Adkins, this is all too much." She was herself near to tears.

"It's no more than a trinket," he said, "a token of what I may call. . .perpetuity."

Even as she watched him, fascinated, he slipped her purse from beneath her arm and tucked the jewel into it, returning the purse to where he had got it. "I shall have it back, you see, when I have you."

Mrs. Norris managed to get to her feet. She excused herself and trundled off in the direction of the powder room. But finding first a door to the park, she stepped outside and thanked the good Lord she was a woman who kept her coat on everywhere; it was still about her shoulders. She was all in a piece. She fled along the walk toward Central Park West, and thought she had never seen so lovely a sight as the first empty taxi.

How close she had come to making an utter fool of herself no one must ever know, she thought, except Mr. Adkins, who would in time come to see his share in the proposed folly. She would seek him out in daylight and give him back his jewelry. If she had behaved cowardly tonight, it was to be atoned with at least that much courage on the morrow.

Near home, she treated herself to a strong cup of tea and some toast at a Schrafft's on Madison Avenue. She preferred, reaching home to take the shame she could not quite keep down, directly to her own room.

Ah, but a welcome sight was Mr. Jamie, despite the scowl with which he greeted her. He was still in the black mood, and that was all right, she thought. It was a great relief after the giddy, grinning Romeo from whom she had fled.

"Your dentist called," Jimmie said with a considerable edge to his voice.

"My dentist," she repeated, managing at the last second to keep the wonder from her voice, and added lamely: "I have a bad tooth."

"Three times within the hour," he said. "Have you that many bad teeth?"

36

Monday morning found Jasper Tully making out a library call-slip for The Sando Bugle.

It was the rare librarian who made an editorial comment, but Tully got one. "Getting homesick, are you?" the man said, taking the detective for an outlander.

Tully was pleased, somehow, that the brand of New York City wasn't on him. "Yeah," he drawled, "I guess I am. Anybody else coming here to read *The Bugle*?"

"Sure, lots of people. Everybody comes to New York."

"That's a damn lie," Tully said, and stalked across the room to the table where he waited for *The Bugle* to be delivered to him. He learned two things from his morning's reading which he thought concerned him: the murderer had been able to check

Murdock the Mighty's itinerary in *The Bugle,* and thereby set up his alibi when Ellie True was killed. And in a few issues of the earlier year, the magician's advertisements had appeared alongside the account of the murder of Mrs. Bellowes.

And Tully learned one thing which he did not think concerned him, the Sando activity Joe had mentioned: the valley coal mines going over to the ownership of the Tripp Gold Mining Company.

It might concern him at that, Tully realized, inasmuch as it might account for the amount of cash the Widow Bellowes had available when her phony doctor showed up a few months later.

And still he didn't have what took the murderer to Sando in the first place. Or did he? Back at the office he again called the Sando police.

"What I'd like for you to get me, Joe—the names of all the strangers who came down to Sando on that Bellowes Mine deal. And here's the big thing—are you listening?—I want to know if the Widow Bellowes did any entertaining of them, and just who she entertained if she did."

"I'll get it if it's gettable," Joe said. "Don't suppose you could send for me to come to New York if I get something good?"

"Maybe it could be arranged," Tully said.

"I don't want to fly. I want to come into...Grand Central Station!"

"Sure, Joe," Tully said. He didn't have the heart to tell him that coming from Southern Ohio, he was going to land in the Pennsylvania Station.

37

Jimmie was waiting at Mr. Wiggam's door when the older man arrived at the office.

"I want to see you," Wiggam said, as though Jimmie were there for some other purpose.

Once in the door, however, Jimmie took the offensive. "I think we should drop the Adkins case, sir. But if I can't convince you of that, I feel I must insist that you take an equal share in its preparation with me."

"Interesting," Wiggam said, eyeing his calendar.

"I think our Mr. Theodore Adkins is schizoid."

Wiggam made his usual impatient gesture with the lingo of psychiatry.

Jimmie plunged on. "Just how far gone he is, I don't know."

"Surely you don't mean he's dangerous?"

"I'm not prepared to say that at all, sir. And I don't think it's our concern at the moment."

"I'm glad to hear you say that."

"What I do think concerns us—how do you try a case in which you cannot know beforehand where you stand? This man is unknowable, at least to non-medicos, and I'm fairly sure to himself as well. He may be acting in good faith with us—though I have my doubts of that. But just how he behaved with this Thayer woman we have no way of knowing in advance of public hearing..."

Mr. Wiggam held up his hand. "You can stop spouting, Jim. I'm not displeased to see this streak of Puritanism in you..."

Jimmie swore a most unpuritanical oath under his breath.

"But it so happens," Wiggam went on, "I spent last evening with Mrs. Adkins myself. She and her son have decided they will settle the suit outside of court after all."

"How nice," Jimmie said, the anger following last upon relief. "Lack of confidence in their legal representation, I presume."

"I doubt that has anything to do with it. They rather liked you."

"Thanks," Jimmie said.

"Theodore is going to marry—with this thing out of the way."

"Not Miss Thayer then," Jimmie said with thin sarcasm.

"An older woman, and according to his mother, a woman of independent means. It is understandable that financial independence should be mentioned in this instance. The important thing to Georgianna—that her boy settle down. She considers it inevitable that he marry someone a few years his senior, his having been the baby of the family..."

"For fifty-five years," Jimmie said.

"Mmm, yes." It surprised Wiggam every time he thought of it, too. "It does make one wonder about the 'older' woman, doesn't it?"

"Yes, sir."

"No doubt you're right about him," Wiggam said then. "The quicker this other affair is settled the better for us. You are authorized to pay up to one hundred thousand dollars."

Just like that, Jimmie thought, quite as though Teddy had fathered the little bastard. "May I ask, sir, where the money will come from?"

"The estate; out of capital, I'm afraid."

"As a broker, does Teddy handle any part of the estate?"

"Good heavens, no."

"By which you mean he's not a good business man," Jimmie suggested.

"Not. . .orthodox. I suppose that's the best word. A few years ago he was nominal manager of the estate. He came very near ruining it, trying to buy up coal mines all over the country—to balance the gold mine stock in the family. I forget just how he explained his theory: ingenious presentation—male and female, gold and coal. Utter nonsense, of course. We got out of it without too much loss."

"I suppose the coal was female in his theory?" Jimmie mused aloud.

"Naturally," Wiggam said, and in a way that suggested a certain sympathy with that aspect of Adkins' theory.

38

As soon as Mrs. Norris finished the most essential of chores that morning, she dressed herself in her black suit, and transferred the contents of her blue purse to her black one, including the lover's knot. She had put her hand into the purse, half-hoping that it would not be there, that the whole business with Mr. Adkins had occurred in the night's dreaming. But it was there: she felt the bow shape of it within the handkerchief. She would as soon have looked upon a tarantula.

Finding Mr. Adkins' Wall Street address in the phone book, she decided to go directly to his office. It would be easier to face him there, where presumably secretaries and clerks would be within earshot of any too-loud protests.

A Gentleman Called

She rode downtown on the Lexington subway, got off at Broadway, and walked thence to the office building. She did love this part of the city, its narrow streets, its sudden reversions to olden landmarks amid the skyscrapers. How she would enjoy it, this dread mission accomplished. Really he had behaved impossibly. He must be a bit off.

And what about herself?

Well. She was through the "A's" without finding an Adkins in the building directory.

Now that was very curious. She went to the elevator starter. He had not heard of such a tenant in the building. But there were several brokerages. She might try them. Mrs. Norris did—without turning up Mr. Theodore Adkins, though a few people thought they had heard the name.

Mrs. Norris went down to the public telephones and again looked up the address. It was given as she had taken it. She wrote down the phone number also. Then she called it. After two rings a woman answered:

"Where are you?" Mrs. Norris asked.

"This is Mr. Adkins' answering service. Mr. Adkins is not in his office at the moment. Can I have him call you?"

"But where is his office?" Mrs. Norris demanded.

"I cannot tell you, madam."

"And why not?"

"I do not know where it is. One moment, please." She came back on the phone a few seconds later and gave Mrs. Norris the Wall Street address where she now was.

"Thank you," she said and hung up. A perfect circle. She

had no choice herself but to turn tail and go home to her work, and some cogitation.

By the time she got back to the apartment, however, she had decided on another, bolder tack. She called the business office of the telephone company.

"I'm calling for Jasper Tully of the District Attorney's office," she said, for she knew that as a private citizen she would get precious little information. "I want the address of this phone listing. I want to know where you send the bill."

She gave the Whitehall number and waited, and heard her own heartbeat mark the long wait.

The operator returned. "The bill is sent to Mr. Theodore Adkins, Box Z-22, Wall Street Station."

"Why is the number listed in the phone book to a Wall Street office address?"

"It would be the address the customer gave us, madam. Do you wish to speak to the supervisor?"

"I do," Mrs. Norris said. An answering service, she reasoned, answered only when you didn't answer yourself after a given number of rings. She again identified herself as Tully's assistant. "Whitehall 9-7150," she said then, "I want to know where it rings."

A few seconds later the supervisor returned and gave her the Wall Street address. Then she added: "The phone also rings at an unlisted address—732 East 61st Street."

"Thank you," Mrs. Norris said with authority.

She had no more than hung up and looked at the clock to see that it was ten minutes to eleven than the musicless bray of the house phone quivered the stillness. It was the doorman.

"Your boy friend is on the way up," he said.

"Did you tell him I'm home?"

"He didn't ask."

"I'm too busy to let anyone in," she said. "I won't answer the door."

"'Atta girl."

Mrs. Norris listened out the buzzing of the hall door. And she thought all the long painful seconds how silly it was not to open the door enough to at least hand through his jewel to him. But she somehow knew that he would get in, and that she would not persuade him here. It was better to seek him out in his own lair. There she could leave when she was ready. What a situation. And him a client of Mr. James'!

Once more the house phone rang. She did not answer it. Some moments later she heard a tap on the door and the doorman called in: "He's gone. Left a note for you I'm tucking under the door."

Mrs. Norris came out from the kitchen and got it after the man was gone. She wanted no conversation with him either.

Mr. Adkins had written a page as neat as the face of a clock:

Dearest one,

Do not avoid me, but if you must until your heart tells you, I await your word. Call me at Whitehall 9-7150. You may leave a discreet message with my office. I will come.

Bless you, my jewel.

Treasure the lover's knot I gave you. My life is bond for it.

T.A.

39

"I don't think I should even talk to you without my lawyer, Mr. Jarvis."

Daisy Thayer was batting her jewel-trimmed eyes at him. Jimmie knew she was going to talk to him, and by her own preference without a third party present. "I'll go over all the legal aspects of the matter with him, Miss Thayer," he said.

"You're sweet," she said. "I always knew my friend had good taste, but I didn't know it got as far as picking out a lawyer."

Jimmie felt like something on a bargain counter.

"Mr. Jarvis, I feel terribly conspicuous sitting here..." They were in the public lounge of Mark Stewart's department store. "Couldn't we go somewhere else to talk?"

"Certainly," Jimmie said.

"Will you take me to lunch?"

"I'll buy you a drink," Jimmie said. "I'm sorry but I have an engagement for lunch."

Daisy got up by degrees, leaving her fingers to the last moment on Jimmie's arm. "You aren't a bit sorry, sugar," she said. "But meet me at Purple Pete's on 35th Street. You can see it from the corner."

Jimmie watched her out of sight. She was scarcely real, but she was about to get a very real sum of money—on which she had probably been counting since the age of sixteen. Jimmie lit a cigarette and thought about Miranda and her theory: that Teddy had connived with this woman to the purpose of breaking the old lady's hold on his inheritance. Seeing Daisy, Jimmie thought it not nearly so far-fetched. Nobody, not even Teddy Adkins, could enter any sort of relationship with Daisy Thayer without knowing what she was up to...gold and coal...ha!

Teddy had not "fallen for her," as tradition understood the phrase. Of that Jimmie was sure. He, too, had gone into the affair with calculation. Perhaps the "older woman" suddenly brought forth now had been waiting all the while in the wings, just waiting for this little curtain raiser to be rung down—for The Cracking of Mama's Safe.

It was going to be fun—as soon as he got offstage himself—to sit back and watch the major drama, Jimmie decided. Reluctantly he put out his cigarette and forsook the public lounge. He was very fond of public places for private thinking—Forty-second Street, Grand Central Station, Herald Square. He paused there to watch the clock strike and then hastened on to Purple Pete's where Daisy was already waiting for him.

"A rendezvous," Jimmie said, crawling into the booth opposite her.

"I always feel wicked having a drink at noon," Daisy said.

"You should never do anything more wicked," Jimmie said. "Miss Thayer, I'm prepared to offer quite a sum of money on behalf of my client—if you agree that it should not be a matter for public arbitration."

There was not a bat to her eye now. "That's entirely up to my lawyer, Mr. Jarvis. I don't think it's proper of you even to come to me about it."

"I'm not an altogether proper fellow," Jimmie said.

"You would be with a girl like me," Daisy said deep in her throat.

Jimmie laughed, and not entirely in merriment. "I intend to put it up to your lawyer, Miss Thayer, but it occurred to me there might be certain aspects to the whole thing which he might not be familiar with."

"Such as?"

"Well, I might say your sentimental attachment to my client's army identification tag—and all that charity work you did for the blood bank a while back."

"My own inclination would be to settle," Daisy said, "for my son's sake. . ."

"Naturally," Jimmie said.

"Don't you be so 'natural,' Mr. Jarvis. I could say plenty about that client of yours. He was a deceiving man, as well as breaking his promises to me."

"Did he promise to marry you, Miss Thayer?"

"If he hadn't—I wouldn't have done the things. . .I did."

"And yet," Jimmie said quietly, "you knew all the time that he was deceiving you."

"I don't know what you mean," Daisy said.

"Cardova—wasn't that the name he gave you?"

"I don't know whatever you're talking about, Mr. Jarvis."

Jimmie turned his glass around. There was no reason for the girl from the Credit Department to have made up that story. Daisy was lying. "Drink up," he said. "It's time to go and see a lawyer, yours."

Daisy moistened her lips. "Wherever did you hear a story like that, Mr. Jarvis?"

"I didn't make it up," Jimmie said. "But I'll tell it to your attorney. Let's go."

"I have to go back to Mark Stewart's," Daisy protested.

"Honey, you aren't ever going back to Mark Stewart's and you know it."

40

Tommy Bassett couldn't get back to the office fast enough. Tully had assigned him the chore of looking up Tripp Gold Mines. He had something and he knew it.

"Hey, Mr. Tully," he started spouting at the door, "do you know who owns all that stock—the T. H. Adkins estate."

Tully leaned back and groped for his empty pipe. It was his one gesture of excitement. "Adkins. . .the philanthropist who broke down the Ellie True case. I don't suppose you got a picture of him, Tommy?"

"No, sir, but I'll go and look."

"Not now, lad. I may need you here. Any other information on him?"

"It's just the financial records I looked up, stuff on the

estate." He consulted his notes. "It's administered by the legal firm of Johnson, Wiggam and Jarvis."

Only a new brightness came into Tully's eyes. "Get Mr. Jarvis on the phone for me, Tommy."

"Yes, sir. . .oh-h-h." Tommy's explanation sounded like a groan.

"What's the matter?"

"It was him I called yesterday, wasn't it?" Tully nodded. "That's where he was, Mr. Tully, at the Adkins' home in Connecticut."

Tully frowned. "Get him," he repeated and pointed to the phone.

Meanwhile the call came through from the Sando police. "I got a half-dozen names for you," Joe said. "The widow had 'em all up to the house a couple of times."

"Adkins," Tully said. "Is there a Theodore Adkins on the list?"

"T. E. Adkins," Joe said. "Could that be him?"

"Could be," Tully said. "It very well could be. Thanks, Joe. I'll keep you informed."

Bassett reported that Mr. Jarvis was not in his office. Nor was there any answer to his home phone.

41

Mrs. Norris, not wanting the doorman to know any more of her business, took the service elevator down and went out through the basement. Walking the few blocks to East Sixty-first Street, she had time to consider some of the untruths Mr. Adkins had told her. In his note he had mentioned his office. A lie that: no one in the building had any knowledge of his ever having had an office there.

    He must be the heir to the fortune, of course: Mr. James said so. What she really wondered was whether it might not be her own particular feeling about money, specifically about the money she had worked for and saved, which colored her impression. The truth was she had now the distinct feeling that his entire performance had been aimed at extorting her widow's savings. And all by the promise of marriage! Oh, the conceit of the man. It was over that he would stumble some day, unless he learned there were women in the world who could resist him.

She arrived at the 61st Street address. A tenement house! The man must be a complete fraud. Or a miser. But of course that was it! And he was indeed expecting to live off her money. The Wall Street phone listing gave him an important address for the price of an answering service.

She stood a moment outside the bleak and foreboding hallway and looked up at the faded brick front. What eyes might be looking down upon her from behind the gray curtains, the dust-blotted windows. Some might call him eccentric, but for the first time, Mrs. Norris felt a little afraid of the man. She decided to go home, coward or no. Whirling round from the entrance, however, she caught sight of Mr. Adkins, bounding across the street to her with a smile on his face like the slice of an orange.

He must, she realized, have followed her all the way from Fifth Avenue, and that in turn meant he must have watched her apartment building from the corner until she came out, suspecting her use of the service door. All she could do at the instant was stand in her tracks till he reached her.

"Oh, my dear, I am delighted you have found me!" he cried.

"I inquired of the phone company..." she started to explain in random quest of escape through conversation.

But he had her firmly by the arm, the key already in his hand. "What matter? Love can always find the way."

It was impossible to be afraid of him, only annoyed with his persistence. "Mr. Adkins I only wanted to give you my answer."

"You will give me nothing on the street."

"It's not proper," she protested, "to go into your house."

"My dear," he said, and let go of her arm, having her by then at the stairwell. "I shouldn't dream of closing my apartment door. Stop acting ridiculous. We shall have a cup of tea—in view of all the neighbors who pass, and I assure you they will be numerous—and to accomplish anything as even slightly improper as an unmarried kiss, we should have to move far more quickly than either you or I are capable of doing."

The reasonableness of this speech did indeed make her protest seem ridiculous. It was very hard at such a moment to connect him with the romantic flibberty-gibbit he made of himself at other times. She might even keep him settled long enough to convince him she had no intention of accepting his proposal of marriage. And if she could not she would leave the jewel and go. She allowed herself to follow him up the stairs.

42

After a conference between James Jarvis and himself, Daisy Thayer's lawyer assured her it was all right to talk to Jimmie.

"Everything?" Daisy said, as though it were not the safe thing to do at all.

"Everything he wants to know."

"I think you two are conspiring against me," Daisy said. "I never made easy money in my life."

"And so much of it," her lawyer murmured. "Just tell him everything from the beginning the way you told me."

Daisy told it truthfully this time, so far as Jimmie could tell, starting at the umbrella counter, and she admitted having checked up on Adkins' true identity, and his credit information.

"Why?" said Jimmie.

"Because he told me his name was Alexander G. Cardova, and I didn't believe him. I got lots of friends Italians, and I just knew he wasn't."

"Now tell me why you denied this up till now, Miss Thayer?"

"Because Teddy came to see me after I filed the suit and said he'd see I got something out of it even if I lost—though he was going to try to settle out of court for a lot of money—if I just didn't mention him using the name Cardova."

"Why, I wonder," Jimmie said.

"He said it was the name of a good friend of his."

Jimmie accepted the answer, although it struck him as curious: it was the first reference he had ever heard to any friend of Teddy Adkins.

"Well, me getting to know him so well," Daisy went on, "and him promising to marry me when I knew he wasn't even using his own name—I just did the only thing I could about it, Mr. Jarvis—the baby."

Jimmie glanced at her lawyer. He was apparently in blithe ignorance of just how Daisy had gone about that. But then he had never met Teddy Adkins.

"Anyway, he told me he was an inventor, and then in the end it was at the point of me loaning him some money for his inventions to get patents. And since I knew there was money where he came from I figured I didn't have much to lose."

"How much did you have to lose, Miss Thayer, in cash, I mean?"

"Almost three thousand dollars though I told him it was five which was what he wanted."

"Five?" Jimmie repeated.

"That's what he asked for," Daisy said.

Jimmie was weathering a bit of shock. Five thousand dollars was the amount Teddy had to clear to contribute to his mother's support.

"Did he take the three thousand?" he asked.

"Well, I gave it to him that night just before bedtime. He was kind of pettish about it not being all I said it was. But everything blew up that night. . .later. He was real sweet at first. Gave me the prettiest little gold pin—a fleur-de-lis—do you know what that is?"

Jimmie nodded.

"But in the middle of the night when he thought I was sleeping he got up and dressed, quiet as a worm. I let him go till I heard him in my dressing table drawer. I thought the dirty little bum wasn't only taking my three thousand dollars, but he was taking back his jewel, and aiming to walk out on me and he didn't think I was ever going to find Mr. Alexander G. Cardova."

Jimmie leaned forward, fascinated.

Daisy herself warmed to the story she was telling. "When he was all set—and mind you it was just about pitch dark in the room—only the light from the street shining in. He must've studied that room like braille the way he got round. When he was all set, he came to the side of the bed, and gentle as a lamb, he pulled down the sheet and put his cold fingers just as delicate—on my cheek and on my throat and on my breast. It made me shiver so I had to speak up. I said then: 'Is this supposed to be goodbye, Mr. Theodore Adkins?' I could hear the echo of my own voice in that room."

"It must have given him a shock," Jimmie said.

"He jumped like a cricket," Daisy said. "He sat down at the bottom of the bed and I could hear him panting for breath. 'As a matter of fact, my dear, that is exactly what it was supposed to be,' he said just as cool. So I got pretty cool about it myself. 'Turn on the light, Teddy'—I always did call him that, him saying from the first it was his nickname. 'Turn on the light, and let's talk business.' That was when I told him I was going to have a baby, and if he didn't marry me I'd slap a suit on him for being its father. He just laughed, and didn't believe me till last week. And I didn't see him ever since till that night last week."

"Did he give back the money?"

"He did, and he gave back my gold locket."

"Gold locket?" said Jimmie.

"That's right. That's what he took from my jewel box, a little gold locket. He wasn't taking the fleur-de-lis like I thought. He was intending to leave that as a kind of a souvenir, and taking for a keepsake my little gold locket. But I gave him back the fleur-de-lis."

"All sentiment and no sense, my man," said Jimmie. "That's why we're paying off one hundred thousand dollars."

He left Daisy and her lawyer in an even more thoughtful mood than he had been in when he sought them out. In fact, he was genuinely troubled about Teddy Adkins—the man was at once calculating and irresponsible. He was mercurial—of person and of tongue, tripping off lies more easily than the truth, and moving so fast from one point to the next, even his lies had difficulty in catching up with him.

Jimmie was nearer to his home than he was to the office. And home was the point from which he had had all his dealings with Teddy Adkins. He boarded a Fifth Avenue bus and sat back remembering Adkins' first visit to the house. Afterwards Jimmie had gone into the kitchen where Mrs. Norris was entertaining Jasper Tully and asked her if she thought Adkins was a lady's man. What was it she had said that Tully took with ill grace—she thought him attractive.

A great number of things then broke in upon Jimmie's train of thought at once—Tully's own assignment of that night, its possible tie-in with Marjory Neville's death. He himself could tie Adkins into the Ellie True murder! He rose up in the bus and walked forward as though that would hasten him home. He wanted to see Tully, but he wanted also to take Mrs. Norris along with him as long as he was this close to home.

43

Mrs. Norris was very short of breath by the time she reached the fifth floor walk-up apartment. Mr. Adkins had gone up the stairs like a bouncing ball, at first before her, leading, then aft, encouraging. And once he had the effrontery to say:

"If you'd married me first, love, I might have carried you."

"Ha!" Mrs. Norris said. "It'd take you two trips."

"Possibly," he said, and smiled as though in beatific happiness. He unlocked the apartment door and flung it open. He bowed from the waist, waiting her entry.

Mrs. Norris took her first timid step into a bachelor's apartment. You might call the one she kept for Mr. James that. But it was entirely different. Oh, in so many ways. Mr. Adkins was a gypsy! She had never in her life been in a place like this:

hung with tapestries and masks, lined with clay model heads. And pictures of costumes were hung round the walls, and the costumes themselves, bits of armor, and all sorts of weapons.

"It's a museum!" she cried.

Adkins stood, his hands on his hips, his elbows out, resembling a spinning top in the little sway of his body. Mrs. Norris wondered if it was herself that was a bit dizzy.

"You, my dear, are the first woman ever to grace it," Adkins said, "the first living woman, that is." And he laughed at his own macabre joke.

"What do you do here?"

"I make tea—and effigies." He put two bricks to the door, one to keep it open a certain width, and one to keep it closed that width. "Come. I've kept my word. The door is open, and there are a dozen heads in the building of a size to peek round that corner, so fear not for your modesty. I have something to show you." He led her to a stand amid the tables and pedestals (on which were models of women's heads and in some instances, busts of women) and at the stand unswathed some brown, dirty clothes, revealing in wet clay a bust of...well, she supposed it was herself, but in oh, such a nasty mood.

"I wouldn't want to see that in a mirror," she said bluntly.

Mr. Adkins smiled. "You could pay me no higher compliment. When people show themselves to me at what they propose as their best, I see them at their worst."

She flicked a finger about the room. "Who are all of them?"

"Are you jealous?" he said, with an impish twinkle in his eye. "I'll banish them." And with a sweep of his arm he toppled two of the nearest clay models to the floor. They made a great thud, but nary a lip nor an ear nor a nose so much as chipped.

Mrs. Norris could not but titter at the indestructibility of his women. Watching her, Mr. Adkins puckered his face into a blue wrath. He caught from the wall a primitive axe and began hacking wildly at the toppled models, all of which merely moved and spun, and shed little more of themselves than dust, until finally the axe-head flew from its handle, and hurtling through the air, grazed Mrs. Norris' brow—or so she thought. She saw the flick of stone and felt a sharp pain. Because she could still see for an instant thereafter, a watery shimmering view of the strange room and man, she thought it must be but a glancing blow. But then there was nothingness.

44

Jimmie turned the key in the door and called out Mrs. Norris' name as soon as he opened it. There was no answer. He went to the foyer table where she was in the habit of leaving him a note if she expected to be out at an unexpected hour. But this was not an unexpected hour for her to be out. The only unexpected thing about it was the dust on the polished table.

Jimmie went through the house, somehow hoping she would come home while he was there. There was, he thought, something about the place which bespoke a hasty departure, either that or a limited occupancy. For example, there was not a thing in the huge refrigerator to indicate her usual early shopping.

On his way out of the building, he asked the doorman if Mrs. Norris had by any chance mentioned to him where she was going.

"Isn't she up there?" the man said. "She was a few minutes ago, sir."

"She's not now," Jimmie said. "Thanks, John."

"She must have gone out through the basement then," John said after him.

Jimmie turned back. "Why would she do that?"

John took off his glove and rubbed his chin. "Mr. Jarvis, I wouldn't want it to get back to her that I told you, sir, but that little man's been here already today—the little bald one who always comes to see you before you get home?"

Jimmie nodded.

"Well, sir, he was here this morning—not an hour ago—and I called up the way I always do to inform her who's coming up whether they asked to be announced or no. And he's not been asking it lately..."

Jimmie made a gesture of impatience. He was now remembering Teddy Adkins' "older woman." But Mrs. Norris had sense, he told himself, and she had Jasper Tully...or did she have as much of either as he had thought?

"She said she wasn't going to answer the door to him, and it was the first time she didn't tell me to keep my nose out of her affairs."

"Go on," Jimmie said.

"He went up and he came down, and I don't think he saw her," John said, "for he went to the table in there in the vestibule and wrote a note which he asked me to give her personally. I took it up and when she wouldn't answer to me either, I tucked it under the door."

There had been no note on the floor, Jimmie knew that. He signaled a cab to wait for him. "Anything else, John?"

"Do you think he's up to no good, the same as I do, sir?" the old doorman said. "Your Mrs. Norris is too nice a lady for him."

"I agree on both things," Jimmie said.

"Then I'll tell you something I should be ashamed of. But I felt the way you do. I read the note, sir. It was full of mush and promises."

"Oh, Godalmighty," Jimmie said.

45

When Jasper Tully swore, it was with rare deliberation and thoroughness. He now delivered a veritable litany against the day he had ever allowed Annie Norris to think herself a detective.

"Do you think she's trying to bring this man to justice herself? Is that it?" said Jimmie.

"What else? Of course, that's what she's doing," Tully said.

Jimmie had his doubts, though he kept them to himself. But having briefly compared notes with Tully, he did not consider that possibility to be any more dangerous than trying to marry Teddy Adkins. "He has an office on Wall Street; did you try it?"

"He's not expected there till this afternoon," said Tully. "Bassett just checked."

"And he was at my apartment within the hour," Jimmie said.

Tully began to pace his office. "I suppose we'd better try to pick up her trail from her own back door." He bellowed down the hall. "Tommy!"

Bassett came running and Tully gave him his instructions. "Call in every half hour wherever you are."

"A half hour's a long time," Jimmie said. He picked up the phone and called the Adkins house in Connecticut. He asked for Miranda, wondering while he waited, who would break the ultimate news of her brother to her.

All that Miranda could suggest by way of finding him was that Jimmie leave a message with Teddy's secretary.

"The Precinct men are staking out his office," Tully said. "Oh, I hope the devil takes a feather to her for this."

A call came through from the stake-out. Theodore Adkins had no office at that address on Wall Street.

Tully picked up the notation of Adkins' phone number. "Who the devil did Bassett talk to then?"

Jimmie was already dialing the number. He could tell instantly it was an answering service.

Tully got the telephone supervisor on the line. "I want information on Whitehall 9-7150," he said, having identified himself. "It seems to be listed to a dummy address."

"It's a dual phone service as I explained to your office this morning, sir..."

"Hold it," Tully said. "Who did you talk to in our office?"

"I'm sure I don't know her name. She said she was calling for you, sir."

"All right," Tully said. "Just give me the information again."

"The residential address which that number also services is 732 East 61st Street."

"Thank you very much," Tully said, hanging up, getting to his feet and holstering his gun all in the same instant. "There! She was even trying to get that information through to me," he said to Jimmie. "I told you what she was doing." He put his hat on his head and led the way out, loping down the hall like a rheumatic moose.

46

When Mrs. Norris came to, she found herself propped and cushioned like the Queen of Sheba. Mr. Adkins was waving a scented cloth beneath her nose, and he seemed to have half-drowned her with compresses, for her head and shoulders were soaking.

"Bless you," he cried. "You are alive!"

"I'm very glad one of us is aware of it," she said, and looking painfully about, she recalled the situation. "Help me off this couch at once, sir. You've closed the door, Mr. Adkins."

"I bolted it, as a matter of fact. How is it our song goes: 'Get up and bar the door?' I did just that. And since there is to be no marriage ceremony, we can at least have a marriage feast in private. Look, I'm binding your head in what might have been a bridal wreath."

"When did that news get through to you?" Mrs. Norris said of his abandoning his matrimonial prospects.

Teddy Adkins was too busy to answer. He thrust a mirror into her hand. Her head, as she watched—and assumed it to be her head—became swathed and circled in silken handkerchiefs he was pulling out of a bottle by the dozens. Then turning the bottle upside down, he extracted from there a fistful of red poppies which he flung about her. Mad! Out of his head—or she out of hers?

"You did not know I was a magician!" he cried. "Did you not ever hear of Murdock the Mighty?"

"You're acting daft, man."

"Dear Mrs. Norris, how many people would agree with you if only they knew me as well. But I am not known at all, for I am many people. I am he, and he, and he. . ." He pointed to one, then another of the pictures on the wall, amongst which Mrs. Norris could see very little resemblance, except perhaps in the general tendency to rotundity.

"Are they all you?" she said, unable herself to match them. But then at the moment she could not have matched one of her own eyes with the other.

"All, every one. . .and all these ladies. . ." He rubbed his chin. "We might call them your ladies-in-waiting, my dear. . .they were the brides-to-be of those various gentlemen." He began to make the round of his sculptured heads. "Do you not remember her? This is Ellie True."

"The Murder of Ellie True!" Mrs. Norris cried. She remembered.

Mr. Adkins bowed. "Your humble servant." He swung around and made a face at as ugly a lump of clay as Mrs. Norris could imagine. "This is the Widow Bellowes. I swear her to have been the devil's midwife. But I don't suppose you would have known her."

Mrs. Norris had no notion now what she did or didn't know. She had always thought him a bit daft in a pleasant sort of way. And he was cheerful enough in public to be morbid in his privacy—but to have created a studio like this for himself: it was like furnishing your own room in the underworld!

"You don't take me seriously, do you?" he said.

"Surely not as seriously as you take yourself, Mr. Adkins."

"Then perhaps you would like to meet the most recent amour. The clay, you will observe, is not yet dry. Her name is Arabella Sperling. And there—" he darted a finger at one of the pictures—"that dapper chap with briefcase and umbrella. . .I wonder would you have observed his name in the vestibule? Alexander Cardova. She finally found in him a lover, Arabella did, and I must say that of them all, she most deserved him."

Mrs. Norris managed to pump herself out of his cushions. Her legs would not support her, however, so she sat down on the edge of the nearest chair. "I don't care much for your hobby, Mr. Adkins," she said with as much dignity as she could muster. "But I would appreciate the cup of tea you offered, thank you. Then I will let you see me home."

"My dear, you are home!" He pulled up a chair and sat down, his knees touching hers. "Do you know, Mrs. Norris," he went on quite earnestly, and his eyes as sharp as darts, "you are the only woman I have ever known whom I have found it genuinely difficult to loathe?"

"Get up from there and let me go," she said, "or I'll make it simple for you now. I've never heard anything so conceited in my life. Do you think all you have to do is propose yourself as a giddy rogue and any woman will marry you?"

"You are my only refusal," he said.

"And what do you call that Daisy Thayer?"

"Why, I quit her, dear woman! She'd be Mrs. Adkins now if I'd have her."

"Is she here?" Mrs. Norris asked suddenly.

"Certainly not. And for an obvious reason."

"What's that?"

Mr. Adkins sighed wearily. "I shall have to do her with two heads, if ever." He threw his arms in the air in a sudden change of mood. "You've not understood me at all."

"I want to go home," Mrs. Norris said. "Nothing like this has ever happened to me before."

"It's all gone wrong," he said, almost tearfully. "I wanted us to be happy in our last hour together. Well, the tea. It can be postponed no longer. The bitter tea of Dr. Woodling. I don't suppose you've heard of him either?"

"Not to my knowledge."

"The murderer of the Widow Bellowes."

"You're a very morbid man, Mr. Adkins," she said after

him. "A little interest in murders is all right, but you've taken an overdose of it."

He smiled wistfully from the kitchen door. "Go and pretty yourself up. There are towels—and a comb. I've mussed the part in your hair, I'm afraid."

"It's hard to make a straight one with an axe," she said.

When she came out from the bathroom, the tea was ready, the steam rising in the chilly room. Mr. Adkins rubbed his hands together in apparent satisfaction at the service he had set. He bounded to her side and held the chair. She was of a mind to open the door, but really for tea it mattered little, and she was very tired.

Mr. Adkins sat beside her, very proper, and poured two cups. He made light of the shuffle of feet and a sudden commotion somewhere down the hall. But almost instantly there was a pounding on the door and the roar of men's voices.

"Open up, Adkins!"

"Cardova or whatever you call yourself!"

"Mrs. Norris are you in there? Are you all right?"

"Why, that's Mr. James," she said.

Adkins lifted his eyes to her face very slowly. "I am disappointed in you," he said. "I thought you a woman as bold as myself, and as circumspect, and here you have invited an army..."

"In the name of the law..."

"That's Jasper Tully!" Mrs. Norris said.

"Then for heaven's sake get up and open the door!" Adkins cried.

Mrs. Norris managed to get up although there was a new and awful weakness coming on her with the hindsight. She was determined not to faint. There might be a first time in her life for that, but this was not to be the occasion. She reached the door and pulled open the latch.

Mr. Tully was the first in, bruising her arms with his bony fingers so fearful and fierce were their clutch. He shot his head out from his shoulders like a crusted turtle, to better peer into her face.

"You're a trifle pale," he said, but his tone was bitterly sarcastic. He thrust her into Jimmie's arms and confronted Adkins: "I arrest you, Theodore Adkins, for the murder of Arabella Sperling..."

Mrs. Norris sucked in enough breath to revive her. She pointed to the nearest bit of sculpture. "And Ellie True," she said.

Jimmie took in the room in a glance. "There must be a dozen!" he cried.

"Presently there should have been," Adkins said ruefully. "Will you gentlemen care for tea?"

Tully lifted a cup to his nose. "You didn't have any of this, Mrs. Norris?"

"Certainly not," she said.

Teddy Adkins offered to take the cup from Tully. "Oh, no," the detective said. "This goes into the laboratory, not into you, my bucko."

"I wouldn't dream of touching it now," Adkins said. "I would much rather have missed the day I was born than the days ahead of me. We shall be very busy, you and I, my dear Jarvis. You will accept my retainer?"

Jimmie chose to beg the issue at the moment. He looked down at Mrs. Norris who was leaning rather heavily on his arm. "How long have you been onto him?" he asked.

Mrs. Norris chose to beg that one. "Where's my purse?" she said, and braced herself for the instant Jimmie would let go of her.

It was among the cushions and Jimmie got it for her. She took from it the diamond lover's knot wrapped still in Mr. Adkins' handkerchief. "I suppose this is as good a time as any to give this back," she said.

Tully groaned and clenched his fists. Jimmie grinned. Mr. Adkins took the pin, glanced at it but an instant, and gave it into the detective's outstretched hand.

Mrs. Norris stood eye to eye with Teddy Adkins. "Why didn't you finish me off with the axe? You had the opportunity."

"I am a gentleman, not a butcher," Adkins said. He held his wrists out then to Tully for the handcuffs, and wearing them, turned back once more to Mrs. Norris. "Do you know, my dear, you have made me very happy today? I have just realized that when this is over I shall probably never have to look at another woman all the days of my life."

About the Author

Dorothy Salisbury Davis is a Grand Master of the Mystery Writers of America, and a recipient of lifetime achievement awards from Bouchercon and Malice Domestic. The author of seventeen crime novels, including the Mrs. Norris Mysteries and the Julie Hayes Mysteries; three historical novels; and numerous short stories; she has served as president of the Mystery Writers of America and is a founder of Sisters in Crime.

Born in Chicago in 1916, she grew up on farms in Wisconsin and Illinois and graduated from college into the Great Depression. She found employment as a magic-show promoter, which took her to small towns all over the country, and subsequently worked on the WPA Writers Project in advertis-

About the Author

ing and industrial relations. During World War II, she directed the benefits program of a major meatpacking company for its more than eighty thousand employees in military service. She was married for forty-seven years to the late Harry Davis, an actor, with whom she traveled abroad extensively. She currently lives in Palisades, New York.

THE MRS. NORRIS MYSTERIES

FROM OPEN ROAD MEDIA

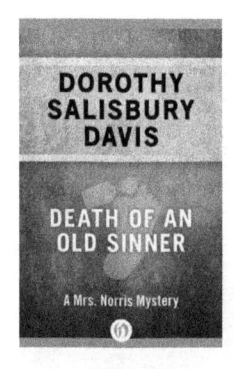

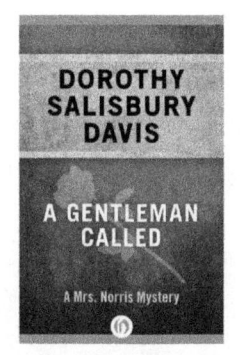

DOROTHY SALISBURY DAVIS
DEATH OF AN OLD SINNER
A Mrs. Norris Mystery

DOROTHY SALISBURY DAVIS
A GENTLEMAN CALLED
A Mrs. Norris Mystery

DOROTHY SALISBURY DAVIS
OLD SINNERS NEVER DIE
A Mrs. Norris Mystery

Available wherever ebooks are sold

OPEN ROAD
INTEGRATED MEDIA

OPEN ROAD
INTEGRATED MEDIA

Open Road Integrated Media is a digital publisher and multimedia content company. Open Road creates connections between authors and their audiences by marketing its ebooks through a new proprietary online platform, which uses premium video content and social media.

Videos, Archival Documents, and New Releases

Sign up for the Open Road Media newsletter and get news delivered straight to your inbox.

Sign up now at
www.openroadmedia.com/newsletters

FIND OUT MORE AT
WWW.OPENROADMEDIA.COM

FOLLOW US:
@openroadmedia and
Facebook.com/OpenRoadMedia